AMERICAN INDIAN
FAIRY TALES

AMERICAN INDIAN FAIRY TALES

Illustrated by John Rae

Derrydale Books
New York • Avenel

First published in 1994 by Derrydale Books,
distributed by
Random House Value Publishing, Inc.,
40 Engelhard Avenue,
Avenel, New Jersey 07001

Random House
New York • Toronto • London • Sydney • Auckland

Designed by Liz Trovato

Printed and bound in Singapore

Library of Congress Cataloging-in-Publication Data
Larned, W. T. (William Trowbridge)
American Indian fairy tales / W.T. Larned ;
illustrated by John Rae.
p. c.m.
ISBN 0-517-10177-7
I. Indians of North America—Legends. 2. Fairy tales—
North America. I. Rae, John, 1882-1963. II. Title.
E98.F6L3 1994
398.2'089'97—dc20
93-46940 CIP AC
8 7 6 5 4 3 2

Contents

Introduction

COME IN AND JOIN Eagle Feather and Morning Glory and the other boys and girls in Iagoo's tent. It's cold outside and the wind is whistling through the branches of the trees. But it's warm in the tent; the fire is blazing. And Iagoo tells wonderful stories. He is the tribe's storyteller, as was his father and his grandfather and his great grandfather.

Iagoo tells stories about things that happened when the world was young, when animals and people lived peacefully together, and there was magic everywhere. With the youngsters who sit close to Iagoo's fire, you will learn about the fierce blustery North Wind, Ka-bib-on-okka, who was outwitted by Shin-ge-bis, the cheerful and courageous fisherman. You will certainly enjoy the story about the rock that rose magically, carrying a brother and sister up among the clouds—and the way the forest creatures, from the largest to the tiniest, tried to get them down.

Iagoo also tells the story of Oweenee, the lovely maiden who married Osseo, a poor and ugly man, and the wonderful adventure they had together. You'll meet the boy who snared the sun and learn how O-jeeg, a mighty hunter, found a way to bring the summer down from the sky when the earth was covered with snow and it was always cold. You'll meet Grasshopper, who one day played one mischievous trick too many, Mish-o-sha, the wicked magician, and Maidwa who went in pursuit of the beautiful red swan.

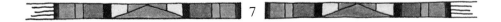

INTRODUCTION

The stories that Iagoo recounts in this book were adopted from the legends collected by Henry R. Schoolcraft. For thirty years, in the first part of the nineteenth century, he lived among the American Indians in the west and around the Great Lakes. In the long evenings, when the storytellers sat at the lodge fires to tell the tales that had been told and retold to generation after generation of boys and girls, Mr. Schoolcraft listened and wrote the stories down, just as he heard them.

The tales in this collection have been retold by W. T. Larned and illustrated by the well-known artist John Rae so that they may delight many more generations of girls and boys.

Now turn the page. Iagoo is ready to begin.

Iagoo,
the Storyteller

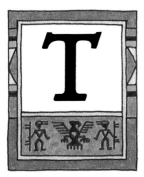

here never was anyone so wise and knowing as old Iagoo. There never was an Indian who saw and heard so much. He knew the secrets of the woods and fields, and he understood the language of birds and beasts. All his life he had lived out-of-doors, wandering far in the forest where the wild deer hide or skimming the waters of the lake in his birch-bark canoe.

Besides the things he had learned for himself, Iagoo knew much more. He knew the fairy tales and the wonder stories told him by his grandfather, who had heard them from *his* grandfather, and so on, way back to the time when the world was young and strange and there was magic in almost everything.

Iagoo was a great favorite with the children. No one knew better where to find the beautiful colored shells that he strung into necklaces for the little girls. No one could teach them so well just where to look for the grasses that their nimble fingers wove into baskets.

For the boys he made bows and arrows—bows from the ash tree, which would bend far back without breaking, and arrows, strong and straight, from the sturdy oak.

But most of all Iagoo won the children's hearts with his stories. Where did the robin get his red breast? How did fire find its way into the wood so that an Indian could get it out again by rubbing two sticks together? Why was Coyote, the prairie wolf, so much cleverer than the other animals? And why was he always looking behind him when he ran? It was old Iagoo who could tell you where and why.

Winter was the time for storytelling. When the snow lay deep on the ground, and North Wind came howling from his home in the Land of Ice, when the cold moon shone from the frosty sky, it was then that the Indians gathered in the wigwam. It was then that Iagoo sat by the fire of blazing logs and the little boys and girls gathered around him.

"Whoo, whoo!" wailed North Wind. The sparks leaped up and Iagoo laid another log on the fire. "Whoo, whoo!" What a mischievous old fellow was this North Wind! One could almost see him—his flowing hair all hung with icicles. If the wigwam were not so strong he would blow it down, and if the fire were not so bright he would put it out. But the wigwam was made for just such a time as this. And the forest nearby had logs to last forever. So North Wind could only gnash his teeth and say, "Whoo, whoo!"

One little girl, more timid than the rest, drew nearer and put her hand on the old man's arm. "Oh, Iagoo," she said, "just listen! Do you think he can hurt us?"

"Have no fear," answered Iagoo. "North Wind can do no harm to anyone who is brave and cheerful. He blusters and makes a lot of noise, but at heart he is really a big coward and the fire will soon frighten him away. Suppose I tell you a story about it."

And the story Iagoo told was the story of how Shin-ge-bis fooled North Wind.

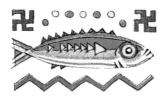

Shin-ge-bis Fools the North Wind

Long, long ago, in the time when only a few people lived upon the earth, there dwelt in the north a tribe of fishermen. The best fish were to be found in the summer season far up in the frozen places where no one could live in the winter at all. For the king of this Land of Ice was a fierce old man called by the Indians Ka-bib-on-okka, North Wind.

Though the Land of Ice stretched across the top of the world for thousands and thousands of miles, Ka-bib-on-okka was not satisfied. If he could have had his way there would have been no grass or green trees anywhere. All the world would have been white from one year's end to another, all the rivers frozen tight, and all the country covered with snow and ice.

Luckily there was a limit to his power. Strong and fierce as he was, he was no match at all for Sha-won-dasee, South Wind, whose home was in the pleasant land of the sunflower. Where Sha-won-dasee dwelt it was always summer. When he breathed upon the land violets appeared in the woods, the wild rose bloomed on the yellow prairie, and the cooing dove called musically to his mate. It was he who caused the melons and the purple grapes to grow. It was he whose warm breath ripened the corn in the fields, clothed the forests in green, and made the earth all glad and beautiful. Then, as the summer days grew shorter in the north, Sha-won-dasee would climb to the top of a hill, fill his great pipe, and sit there—dreaming and smoking. Hour after hour he sat and smoked. And the smoke, rising in the form of a vapor, filled the air with a soft haze until the hills and lakes seemed like the hills and lakes of dreamland. There was not a breath of wind, not a cloud in the sky. There was a great peace and stillness over all. Nowhere else in the world was there anything so wonderful. It was Indian summer.

Now it was that the fishermen who set their nets in the north worked hard and fast, knowing the time was at hand when South Wind would fall asleep and fierce old Ka-bib-on-okka would swoop down upon them and drive them away. Sure enough! One morning a thin film of ice covered the water where they set their nets. A heavy frost sparkled in the sun on the roofs of their huts.

That was sufficient warning. The ice grew thicker, the snow fell in big, feathery flakes. Coyote, the prairie wolf, trotted by in his shaggy white winter coat. Already they could hear a muttering and a moaning in the distance.

"Ka-bib-on-okka is coming!" cried the fishermen. "Ka-bib-on-okka will soon be here. It is time for us to go."

But Shin-ge-bis, the diver, only laughed.

Shin-ge-bis was always laughing. He laughed when he caught a big fish and he laughed when he caught none at all. Nothing could dampen his spirits.

"The fishing is still good," he said to his comrades. "I can cut a hole in the ice and fish with a line instead of a net. What do *I* care for old Ka-bib-on-okka?"

They looked at him with amazement. It was true that Shin-ge-bis had certain magic powers and could change himself into a duck. They had seen him do it and that is why he came to be called "the diver." But how would this enable him to brave the anger of the terrible North Wind?

"You had better come with us," they said. "Ka-bib-on-okka is much stronger than you. The biggest trees of the forest bend before his wrath. The swiftest river that runs freezes at his touch. Unless you can turn yourself into a bear, or a fish, you will have no chance at all."

But Shin-ge-bis only laughed the louder. "My fur coat lent me by Brother Beaver and my mittens borrowed from Cousin Muskrat will protect me in the daytime," he said, "and inside my wigwam is a pile of big logs. Let Ka-bib-on-okka come in by my fire if he dares."

So the fishermen took their leave rather sadly. The laughing Shin-ge-bis was a favorite with them and, the truth is, they never expected to see him again.

When they were gone, Shin-ge-bis set about his work in his own way. First he made sure that he had plenty of dry bark and twigs and pine needles to make the fire blaze up when he returned to his wigwam in the evening. The snow by this time was pretty deep, but it froze so hard on top that the sun did not melt it and he could walk on the surface without sinking at all. As for fish, he well knew how to catch them through the holes he made in the ice. And at night he would go tramping home, trailing a long string of fish behind him, and singing a song he had made up himself:

"Ka-bib-on-okka, ancient man,
Come and scare me if you can.
Big and blustery though you be,
You are mortal just like me!"

It was thus that Ka-bib-on-okka found him, plodding along late one afternoon across the snow.

"Whoo, whoo!" cried North Wind. "What impudent, two-legged creature is this who dares to linger here long after the wild goose and the heron have winged their way to the south? We shall see who is master in the Land of Ice. This very night I will force my way into his wigwam, put his fire out, and scatter the ashes all around. Whoo, whoo!"

Night came. Shin-ge-bis sat in his wigwam by the blazing fire. And such a fire! Each backlog was so big it would last for a moon. (That was the way the Indians, who had no clocks or watches, counted time. Instead of weeks or months, they would say "a moon"—the length of time from one new moon to another.)

Shin-ge-bis had been cooking a fish, a fine fresh fish caught that very day. Broiled over the coals, it was a tender and savory dish and Shin-ge-bis smacked his lips and rubbed his hands with pleasure. He had tramped many miles that day so it was a pleasant thing to sit there by the roaring fire and toast his shins. How foolish, he thought, his comrades had been to leave this place—where fish was so plentiful—so early in the winter.

"They think that Ka-bib-on-okka is a kind of magician," he was saying to himself, "and that no one can resist him. It's my own opinion that he's a man, just like myself. It's true that I can't stand the cold as he does. But then, neither can he stand the heat as I do."

This thought amused him so that he began to laugh and sing:

> "Ka-bib-on-okka, frosty man,
> Try to freeze me if you can.
> Though you blow until you tire,
> I am safe beside my fire!"

He was in such a good humor that he scarcely noticed a sudden uproar that began outside. The snow came thick and fast. As it fell it was caught up again like so much powder and blown against the wigwam, where it lay in huge drifts. But instead of making it colder inside, it was really like a thick blanket that kept the air out.

Ka-bib-on-okka soon discovered his mistake and it made him furious. Down the smoke vent he shouted. And his voice was so wild and terrible that it might have frightened an ordinary man. But Shin-ge-bis only laughed. It was so quiet in that great, silent country that he rather enjoyed a little noise.

"Ho, ho!" he shouted back. "How are you, Ka-bib-on-okka? If you are not careful you will burst your cheeks."

Then the wigwam shook with the force of the blast and the curtain of buffalo hide that formed the doorway flapped and rattled and rattled and flapped.

"Come on in, Ka-bib-on-okka!" called Shin-ge-bis merrily. "Come on in and warm yourself. It must be bitter cold outside."

At these jeering words Ka-bib-on-okka hurled himself against the curtain, breaking one of the buckskin thongs, and made his way inside. Oh, what an icy breath! It was so icy that it filled the hot wigwam like a fog.

Shin-ge-bis pretended not to notice. Still singing, he rose to his feet and threw another log on the fire. It was a fat log of pine and it burned so hard and gave out so much heat that he had to sit a little distance away. From the corner of his eye he watched Ka-bib-on-okka. And what he saw made him laugh again. The perspiration was pouring from his forehead. The snow and icicles in his flowing hair quickly disappeared. Just as a snowman made by children melts in the warm sun of March, so the fierce old North Wind began to thaw! There could be no doubt of it. Ka-bib-on-okka, the terrible, was melting! His nose and ears became smaller, his body began to shrink. If he remained where he was much longer, the king of the Land of Ice would be nothing better than a puddle.

"Come on up to the fire," said Shin-ge-bis cruelly. "You must be chilled to the bone. Come up closer and warm yourselves."

But North Wind had fled, even faster than he came, through the doorway.

Once outside the cold air revived him and all his anger returned. Since he had not been able to freeze Shin-ge-bis, he spent his rage on everything in his path. Under his tread the snow took on a crust. The brittle branches of the trees snapped as he blew and snorted. The prowling fox hurried to his hole. And the wandering coyote sought the first shelter at hand.

Once more he made his way to the wigwam of Shin-ge-bis and shouted down the flue. "Come out," he called. "Come out, if you dare, and wrestle with me here in the snow. We'll soon see who's master then!"

Shin-ge-bis thought it over. "The fire must have weakened him," he said to himself. "And my own body is warm. I believe I can overpower him. Then he will not annoy me any more and I can stay here as long as I please."

Out of the wigwam he rushed and Ka-bib-on-okka came to meet him. Then a great struggle took place. Over and over on the hard snow they rolled, locked in each other's arms.

All night long they wrestled, and the foxes crept out of their holes, sitting at a safe distance in a circle, watching the wrestlers. The effort he put forth kept the blood warm in the body of Shin-ge-bis. He could feel North Wind growing weaker and weaker. His icy breath was no longer a blast, but only a feeble sigh.

At last, as the sun rose in the west, the wrestlers stood apart, panting. Ka-bib-on-okka was conquered. With a despairing wail he turned and sped away. Far, far to the north he sped, even to the land of the White Rabbit. And as he went the laughter of Shin-ge-bis rang out and followed him. Cheerfulness and courage can overcome even the North Wind.

The Little Boy and Girl
in the Clouds

Iagoo, the storyteller, was seated one evening in his favorite corner, gazing into the embers of the log fire like one in a dream.

At such a time the children knew better than to interrupt him by asking questions or teasing him for a story. They knew that Iagoo was turning over in his mind the strange things he had heard and the wonderful things he had seen. They knew that the burning logs and red coals took on curious shapes and made odd pictures that only he could understand and that if they did not disturb him he would soon begin to speak.

On this particular evening, however, although they waited patiently and talked to one another only in low whispers, Iagoo kept on sitting there as if he were made of stone. They began to fear that he had forgotten them and that bedtime would come without a story. So at last little Morning Glory, who was always asking questions, thought of one she had never asked before.

"Iagoo!" she said, and then she stopped, afraid of offending him.

At the sound of her voice the old man roused himself, as if his mind had been away on a long journey into the past.

"What is it, Morning Glory?"

"Iagoo—can you tell me—were the mountains always here?"

The old man looked at her gravely. No matter how hard the question was, or how unexpected, Iagoo was always glad to answer. He never said, "I'm too busy, don't bother me," or "Wait until some other time." So when Morning Glory asked him this very peculiar question, he nodded his wise old head, saying, "Do you know, I've often asked myself that very thing: Were the mountains always here!"

He paused, and looked once more into the fire, as if the answer was to be found there if he only looked long enough. At last he spoke again, "Yes, I think it must be true that the mountains were always here—the mountains and the hills. They were made when the world was made—a long, long time ago. And the story of how the world was made you have heard before. But there is one high hill that was not always here—a hill that grew like magic, all of a sudden. Did I ever tell you the story of the big rock—how it rose and rose and carried the little boy and girl up among the clouds?"

"No, no!" shouted the children in a chorus. "You never told us that one. Tell it to us now."

And this is the story of the magical big rock, as old Iagoo heard it from his grandfather, who heard it from *his* great-grandfather, who was almost old enough to have been there himself when it all happened.

In the days when all animals and men lived on friendly terms, when Coyote, the prairie wolf, was not a bad sort of fellow after you came to know him, and even Mountain Lion would growl pleasantly and pass the time of day with you—there lived in a beautiful valley a little boy and girl.

This valley was a lovely place to live in. Never was there such a playground anywhere on earth. It was like a great green carpet stretching for miles and miles. And when the wind blew upon the long grass it was like looking at the waves of the sea. Flowers of all colors bloomed in the beautiful valley, berries grew thick on the bushes, and birds filled the summer air with their songs.

Best of all, there was nothing whatever to fear. The children could wander at will—watching the gay butterflies, making friends with the squirrels and rabbits, or following the flight of the bee to some tree where his honey was stored.

As for the wild animals, it was all very different from what it is today, when they keep the poor things in cages or coop them up in a little patch of ground behind a high fence. In the beautiful valley the animals ran free and happily, as they were meant to do.

Bear was a big, lazy, good-natured fellow who lived on berries and wild honey in the summer and in winter crept into his cavern in the rocks and slept there until the spring. The deer were not only gentle, but tame as sheep, and often came to crop the tender grass that grew where the two children would play.

They loved all the animals, and the animals loved them. But perhaps their special favorites were Jack Rabbit and Antelope. Jack Rabbit had long legs, and long ears—almost as long as a mule's, and no animal of his size could jump so high. But of course he could not jump as high as Antelope—a beautiful little deer with short horns and slender legs, who could run like the wind.

Another thing that made the happy valley such a pleasant place to live in was the river that flowed through it. All the animals came from miles around to drink from its clear, cool waters and to bathe in it on a hot summer day. One shallow pool seemed made especially for the little boy and girl. Their friend Beaver, with his flat tail like an oar and his feet webbed like a duck's, had taught them how to swim almost as soon as they had learned to walk, and splashing around in the pool on a warm afternoon was among their greatest pleasures.

One day in midsummer the water was so pleasant that they remained in the pool much longer than usual, so that when at last they came out they were quite tired. And also since they were a little chilled, they looked around for a good place where they could get dry and warm.

"Let's climb up on that big flat rock with the moss on it," said the little boy. "We've never done it before. It would be lots of fun."

So he clambered up the side of the rock, which was only a few feet high, and pulled his sister up after him. Then they lay down to rest. Pretty soon, without intending it at all, they were fast asleep.

Nobody knows how it happened that exactly at this time the rock began to rise and grow. But it did happen, because there it is today, high and bare and steep, higher than the other hills in the valley. As the children slept it rose and rose, inch by inch, foot by foot. By the next day it was taller than the tallest trees.

Meanwhile, the children's father and mother were searching for them everywhere, but in vain. There was no trace of them to be found. No one had seen them climb up on the rock, and everyone was much too excited to notice what had really happened to it. The parents wandered far and wide saying, "Antelope, have you seen our little boy and girl? Jack Rabbit, *you* must have seen our little boy and girl." But none of the animals had seen them.

At last they met Coyote, the cleverest of them all, trotting along the valley with his nose in the air. They put the same question to him.

"No," said Coyote. "I have not seen them for a long time. But my nose was given me to smell with and my brains were given me to think with. So who can tell but that I may help you?"

He trotted by their side along the banks of the river. Pretty soon they came to the pool where the children had been swimming. Coyote sniffed and sniffed. He ran around and around with his nose to the ground. Then he ran right up to the rock, put his forepaws up as high as he could reach, and sniffed again.

"H-m-m!" he grunted. "I cannot fly like Eagle and I cannot swim like Beaver. But neither am I stupid like Bear, nor ignorant like Jack Rabbit. My nose has never deceived me yet. Your little boy and girl must be up there on that rock."

"But how could they get there?" asked the astonished parents. For the rock was now so high that the top was lost to sight in the clouds.

"That is not the question," said Coyote severely, unwilling to admit there was anything he did not know. "That is not the question at all. Anybody could ask that. The only question worth asking is, How are we to get them down again?"

So they called all the animals together to talk it over and see what could be done. Then Bear said, "If I could only put my arms around the rock I could climb it. But it is much too big for that." And Fox said, "If it were only a deep hole, instead of a high hill, I would be able to help you." And Beaver said, "If it were just a place out in the water I could swim to, I'd show you very quickly."

But since this kind of talk did not take them very far, they decided to try to jump to the top of the rock. There seemed to be no other way and since each one was anxious to do his part, the smallest one was permitted to make the first attempt.

Mouse made a funny little hop, about as high as your hand. Then Squirrel went a little higher. Jack Rabbit made the highest jump of his life and almost broke his back, to no purpose. Antelope gave a great bound in the air, but managed to land on his feet again without doing himself any harm. Finally, Mountain Lion went a long way off, to get a good start, ran toward the rock with great leaps, sprang straight up—and fell and rolled over on his back. He had made a higher jump than any of them, but it was not nearly high enough.

No one knew what to do next. It seemed as if the little boy and girl must be left sleeping forever up among the clouds.

Suddenly they heard a tiny voice saying, "Perhaps if you let *me* try, I might *climb* up the rock."

They all looked around in surprise, wondering who it was that spoke. At first they could see nobody and thought that Coyote must be playing a trick on them. But Coyote was as surprised as anyone.

"Wait a minute. I'm coming as fast as I can," said the tiny voice again. Then Measuring Worm crawled out of the grass. It was a funny little worm that made its way along by hunching up its back and drawing itself ahead an inch at a time.

"Ho, ho!" said Mountain Lion, from deep down in his throat. He always spoke that way when his dignity was offended. "Ho, ho! Did you ever hear of such impudence? If I, a lion, have failed, how can a miserable little crawling worm like you hope to succeed? Just tell me that!"

"It's downright silly," said Jack Rabbit. "That's what it is. I never heard of such conceit."

However, after much talk, they agreed at last that it could do no harm to let him try. So Measuring Worm made his way slowly to the rock and began to climb. In a few minutes he was higher than Jack Rabbit had jumped. Soon he was farther up than Mountain Lion had been able to leap. Before long he had climbed out of sight.

It took Measuring Worm a whole month, climbing day and night, to reach the top of the magic rock. When he got there he awakened the little boy and girl, who were very much surprised to see where they were, and guided them safely down along a path no one else knew anything about. Thus, by patience and perseverance, the weak little creature was able to do something that Bear, for all his size, and Mountain Lion, for all his strength, could never have done at all.

That was a long time ago. Today there are no more lions or bears in the valley and no one ever thinks of them. But everybody thinks of Measuring Worm, because the big rock is still there and the Indians have named it after him. Tu-tok-a-nu-la, they call it. It is a big name indeed for a little fellow, yet by no means too big when you come to think of the big, brave thing he did.

The Child of the
Evening Star

nce upon a time, on the shores of the great lake
Gitchee Gumee, there lived a hunter who had
ten beautiful young daughters. Their hair was
as dark and glossy as the wings of the black-
bird and when they walked or ran it was with
the grace and freedom of the deer in the forest.
Thus it was that many suitors came to court
them—brave and handsome young men,
straight as arrows, fleet of foot, who could travel from sun to sun
without fatigue. They were sons of the prairie, wonderful horsemen
who would ride at breakneck speed without saddle or stirrup. They
could catch a wild horse with a noose, tame him in a magical way
by breathing into his nostrils, then mount him and gallop off as if
he always had been ridden. There were those also who came from
afar in canoes, across the waters of the great lake, canoes which shot
swiftly along, urged by the strong, silent sweep of the paddle.

All of them brought presents with which they hoped to gain the father's favor. Feathers from the wings of the eagle who soars high up near the sun; furs of fox and beaver and the thick, curly hair of the bison; beads of many colors and wampum, the shells that the Indians used for money; the quills of the porcupine and the claws of the grizzly bear; deerskin dressed to such a softness that it crumpled in the hands—these and many other things they brought.

One by one the daughters were wooed and married, until nine of them had chosen husbands. One by one other tents were raised so that instead of the single family lodge on the shores of the lake there were tents enough to form a little village. The country was a rich one and there was game and fish enough for all.

There remained the youngest daughter, Oweenee—the fairest of them all. Gentle as she was beautiful, none was so kind of heart. Unlike her proud and talkative elder sisters, Oweenee was shy and modest and spoke but little. She loved to wander alone in the woods with no company but the birds and squirrels and her own thoughts. What these thoughts were we can only guess, but from her dreamy eyes and sweet expression, one could suppose that nothing selfish or mean or hateful ever came into her mind. Yet Oweenee, modest though she was, had a spirit of her own. More than one suitor had found this out. More than one conceited young man, confident that he could win her, went away crestfallen when Oweenee began to laugh at him.

The truth is Oweenee seemed hard to please. Suitor after suitor came—handsome, tall young men, the handsomest and the bravest in all the surrounding country. Yet this fawn-eyed maiden would have none of them. One was too tall, another too short. One was too thin, another too fat. At least, those were the excuses she gave for sending them away. Her proud sisters had little patience with her. She seemed to be questioning their own taste, for Oweenee, had she said the word, might have gained a husband more attractive than any of theirs. Yet no one was good enough. They could not

understand her, so they ended up despising her as a silly and un-
reasonable girl.

Her father, too, who loved her dearly and wished her to be
happy, was much puzzled. "Tell me, my daughter," he said to her
one day, "is it your wish never to marry? The handsomest young
men in the land have sought you in marriage and you have sent
them all away—often with a poor excuse. Why is it?"

Oweenee looked at him with her large, dark eyes.

"Father," she said at last. "It is not that I am willful. But it seems
somehow as if I had the power to look into the hearts of men. It
is the heart of a man and not his face that really matters. And I have
not yet found one youth who in this sense is really beautiful."

Soon after, a strange thing happened. There came into the little
village an Indian named Osseo, many years older then Oweenee.
He was poor and ugly, too. Yet Oweenee married him.

How the tongues of her nine proud sisters did wag! Had the
spoiled little thing lost her mind? they asked. Oh, well! They always knew she would come to a bad end, but it was pretty hard
on the family.

Of course they could not know what Oweenee had seen at
once—that Osseo had a generous nature and a heart of gold, that
beneath his outward ugliness was the beauty of a noble mind and
the fire and passion of a poet. That is why Oweenee loved him.
Knowing, too, that he needed her care she loved him all the more.

Now, although Oweenee did not suspect it, Osseo was really a
beautiful youth on whom an evil spell had been cast. He was in
truth the son of the king of the Evening Star—the star that shines
so gloriously in the western sky, just above the rim of the earth as
the sun is setting. Often on a clear evening it hung suspended in the
purple twilight like some glittering jewel. So close it seemed, and
so friendly, that the little children would reach out their hands,
thinking that they might grasp it before it was swallowed by the

night, and keep it always for their own. But the older ones would say, "Surely it must be a bead on the garments of the Great Spirit as he walks in the evening through the garden of the heavens."

Little did they know that poor, ugly Osseo had really descended from that star. And when he, too, stretched out his arms toward it, and murmured words they could not understand, they all made fun of him.

There came a time when a great feast was prepared in a neighboring village and all of Oweenee's kinsfolk were invited to attend. They set out on foot—the nine proud sisters, with their husbands, walking ahead, much pleased with themselves and their finery, and all chattering like magpies. But Oweenee walked behind in silence, and with her walked Osseo.

The sun had set. In the purple twilight, over the edge of the earth, sparkled the Evening Star. Osseo, pausing, stretched out his hands toward it, as if imploring pity. But when the others saw him in this attitude they all made merry, laughing and joking and making unkind remarks.

"Instead of looking up at the sky," said one of the sisters, "he had better be looking on the ground. Or else he may stumble and break his neck." Then calling back to him she cried, "Look out! Here's a big log. Do you think you can manage to climb over it?"

Osseo did not answer, but when he came to the log he paused again. It was the trunk of a huge oak tree blown down by the wind. There it had lain for years, just as it fell, and the leaves of many summers lay thick upon it. There was one thing, however, the sisters had not noticed. The tree trunk was not a solid one, but hollow, and so big around that a man could walk inside it from one end to the other without stooping.

But Osseo did not pause because he was unable to climb over it. There was something mysterious and magical in the appearance of the great hollow trunk. He gazed at it a long time, as if he had seen it in a dream and had been looking for it ever since.

"What is it, Osseo?" asked Oweenee, touching him on the arm. "Do you see something that I cannot see?"

But Osseo only gave a shout that echoed through the forest, and he leaped inside the log. Then as Oweenee, a little alarmed, stood there waiting, a man came out from the other end. Could this be Osseo? Yes, it was he—but how transformed! No longer bent and ugly, no longer weak and ailing, but a beautiful youth—vigorous and straight and tall. His enchantment was at an end.

But the evil spell had not been wholly lifted, after all. As Osseo approached he saw that a great change was taking place in his loved one. Her glossy black hair was turning white, deep wrinkles lined her face, she walked with a feeble step, leaning on a staff. Although he had regained his youth and beauty, she had suddenly grown old.

"Oh, my dearest one!" he cried. "The Evening Star has mocked me in letting this misfortune come upon you. Better far had I remained as I was. Gladly would I have borne the insults and laughter of your people rather than you should be made to suffer."

"As long as you love me," answered Oweenee, "I am perfectly content. If I had the choice to make, and only one of us could be young and fair, it is you that I would wish to be beautiful."

Then he took her in his arms and caressed her, vowing that he loved her more than ever for her goodness of heart. And together they walked hand in hand, as lovers do.

When the proud sisters saw what had happened they could scarcely believe their eyes. They looked enviously at Osseo, who was now far handsomer than any one of their husbands and much their superior in every other way. In his eyes was the wonderful light of the Evening Star, and when he spoke all men turned to listen and admire him. But the hard-hearted sisters had no pity for Oweenee. Indeed, it rather pleased them to see that she could no longer dim their beauty and to realize that people would no longer be singing her praises in their jealous ears.

The feast was spread and all made merry except Osseo. He sat like one in a dream, neither eating nor drinking. From time to time he would press Oweenee's hand and speak a word of comfort in her ear. But for the most part he sat there gazing through the door of the tent at the star-besprinkled sky.

Soon a silence fell on all the company. From out of the night, from the dark, mysterious forest, came the sound of music—a low, sweet music that was like, yet unlike, the song sung by the thrush in summer twilight. It was magical music such as none had ever heard, coming, as it seemed, from a great distance and rising and falling on the quiet summer evening. All those at the feast wondered as they listened. And well they might! For what to them was only music was to Osseo a voice that he understood, a voice from the sky itself, the voice of the Evening Star. These were the words that he heard:

"Suffer no more, my son, for the evil spell is broken and hereafter no magician shall work you harm. Suffer no more. For the time has come when you shall leave the earth and dwell here with me in the heavens. Before you is a dish on which my light has fallen, blessing it and giving it a magic virtue. Eat of this dish, Osseo, and all will be well."

So Osseo tasted the food before him and behold! The tent began to tremble, and rose slowly into the air; up, up above the treetops— up, up toward the stars. As it rose the things within it were wondrously changed. The kettles of clay became bowls of silver, the wooden dishes were scarlet shells, while the bark of the roof and the poles supporting it were transformed into some glittering substance that sparkled in the rays of the stars. Higher and higher it rose. Then the nine proud sisters and their husbands were all changed into birds. The men became robins, thrushes, and woodpeckers. The sisters were changed into various birds with bright plumage. The four who had chattered most, whose tongues were always wagging, now appeared in the feathers of the magpie and bluejay.

Osseo sat gazing at Oweenee. Would she, too, change into a bird and be lost to him? The very thought of it made him bow his head with grief. Then, as he looked at her once more, he saw her beauty suddenly restored, while the color of her garments was the color only to be found where the dyes of the rainbow are made.

Again the tent swayed and trembled as the currents of the air bore it higher and higher, into and above the clouds. Up, up, up—until at last it settled gently on the land of the Evening Star.

Osseo and Oweenee caught all the birds and put them in a great silver cage where they seemed quite content in each other's company. Scarcely was this done when Osseo's father, the king of the Evening Star, came to greet them. He was attired in a flowing robe, spun from stardust, and his long white hair hung like a cloud upon his shoulders.

"Welcome," he said, "my dear children. Welcome to the kingdom in the sky that has always awaited you. The trials you have passed through have been bitter, but you have borne them bravely and now you will be rewarded for all your courage and devotion. Here you will live happily. Yet of one thing you must beware."

He pointed to a little star in the distance—a little winking star, hidden from time to time by a cloud of vapor.

"On that star," he continued, "lives a magician named Wabeno. He has the power to dart his rays, like so many arrows, at those he wishes to injure. He has always been my enemy. It was he who changed Osseo into an old man and cast him down upon the earth. Be careful that his light does not fall upon you. Luckily, his power for evil has been greatly weakened, for the friendly clouds have come to my assistance and form a screen of vapor through which his arrows cannot penetrate."

The happy pair fell upon their knees and kissed his hands in gratitude.

"But these birds," said Osseo, rising and pointing to the cage. "Is this also the work of Wabeno, the magician?"

"No," answered the king of the Evening Star. "It was my own

power, the power of love, that caused your tent to rise and bear you hither. It was likewise by my power that the envious sisters and their husbands were transformed into birds. Because they hated you and mocked you, and were cruel and scornful to the weak and the old, I have done this thing. It is not so great a punishment as they deserve. Here in the silver cage they will be happy enough, proud of their handsome plumage, strutting and twittering to their hearts' content. Hang the cage there, at the doorway of my dwelling. They shall be well cared for."

Thus it was that Osseo and Oweenee came to live in the kingdom of the Evening Star and, as the years passed by, the little winking star where Wabeno, the magician, lived grew pale and paler and dim and dimmer, until it quite lost its power to harm. Meanwhile, a little son had come to make their happiness more perfect. He was a charming boy with the dark, dreamy eyes of his mother and the strength and courage of Osseo.

It was a wonderful place for a little boy to live—close to the stars and the moon, with the sky so near that it seemed a kind of curtain for his bed and all the glory of the heavens spread out before him. But sometimes he was lonely and wondered what Earth was like— the Earth his father and mother had come from. He could see it far, far below—so far that it looked no bigger than an orange. And sometimes he would stretch out his hands toward it, just as the little children on Earth stretch out their hands for the moon.

His father had made him a bow, with little arrows, and this was a great delight to him. But still he was lonely and wondered what the little boys and girls on Earth were doing, and whether they would be nice to play with. Earth must be a pretty place, he thought, with so many people living on it. His mother had told him strange stories of that faraway land, with its lovely lakes and rivers, its great green forests where the deer and the squirrel lived, and the yellow rolling prairies swarming with buffalo.

These birds, too, in the great silver cage had come from Earth, he was told. And there were thousands and thousands just like them, as well as others even more beautiful that he had never seen at all. Swans with long, curved necks, that floated gracefully on the waters, whippoorwills that called at night from the woods, the robin redbreast, the dove, and the swallow. What wonderful birds they must be!

Sometimes he would sit near the cage, trying to understand the language of the feathered creatures inside. One day a strange idea came into his head. He would open the door of the cage and let them out. Then they would fly back to Earth and perhaps they would take him with them. When his father and mother missed him they would be sure to follow him to Earth, and then—

He could not quite see just how it would all end. But he found himself quite close to the cage, and the first thing he knew he had opened the door and let out all the birds. Round and round they flew. And now he was half sorry, and a little afraid as well. If the birds flew back to Earth and left him there what would his grandfather say?

"Come back, come back!" he called.

But the birds only flew around him in circles and paid no attention to him. At any moment they might be winging their way to Earth.

"Come back, I tell you" he cried, stamping his foot and waving his little bow. "Come back, I say, or I'll shoot you."

Then, as they would not obey him, he fitted an arrow to his bow and let it fly. So well did he aim that the arrow sped through the plumage of a bird, and the feathers fell all around. The bird itself, a little stunned but not much hurt, fell down and a tiny trickle of blood stained the ground where it lay. But it was no longer a bird, with an arrow in its wing. Instead there stood in its place a beautiful young woman.

Now, no one who lives in the stars is ever permitted to shed blood, whether it be of man, beast, or bird. So when the few drops fell upon the Evening Star everything was changed. The boy suddenly found himself sinking slowly downward, held up by invisible hands, yet ever sinking closer and closer to Earth. Soon he could see its green hills and the swans floating on the water. Until at last he rested on a grassy island in a great lake. Lying there, and looking up at the sky, he could see the tent descending, too. Down it softly drifted, until it in turn sank upon the island. And in it were his father and mother, Osseo and Oweenee—returned to Earth, to live once more among men and women and teach them how to live. For they had learned many things in their life upon the Evening Star and the children of Earth would be better for the knowledge.

As they stood there, hand in hand, all the enchanted birds came fluttering after them, falling and fluttering through the air. Then as each one touched the Earth it was no longer a bird but a human being. Each was a human being, yet not quite as before. For now they were only dwarfs, Little People, or Puk-Wudjies, as the Indians called them. Happy Little People they became, seen only by a few. Fishermen, they say, would sometimes get a glimpse of them dancing in the light of the Evening Star, on a summer night, on the sandy, level beach of the great lake.

The Boy Who Snared the Sun

eep crusted snow covered the earth and sparkled in the light of a wintry moon. The wind had died away. It was very cold and still. Not a sound came from the forest. The only noise that broke the perfect quiet of the night was the cracking of the ice on Big-Sea-Water, Gitche Gumee, which was now frozen solid.

But inside old Iagoo's teepee it was warm and cheerful. The teepee was covered with the thick, tough skin of the buffalo. The winter coat of Muk-wa, the bear, had now become a pleasant soft rug for Iagoo's two young visitors, Morning Glory and her little brother, Eagle Feather. Squatting at their ease on the warm fur, they waited for the old man to speak.

Suddenly a white-footed mouse crept from his nest in a corner and, advancing close to the children, sat up on his hind legs, like a dog that begs for a biscuit. Eagle Feather raised his hand in a threatening way, but Morning Glory caught him by the arm.

"No, no!" she said. "You must not harm him. See how friendly he is and not a bit afraid. There is game enough in the forest for a brave boy's bow and arrow. Why should he spend his strength on a weak little mouse?"

Eagle Feather, pleased with anything that seemed like praise of his strength, let his hand fall.

"Your words are true words, Morning Glory," he answered. "Against Ahmeek, the beaver, or Wau-be-se, the wild swan, it is better that I should measure my hunter's skill."

At this, Iagoo, turning around, broke his long silence.

"There was a time," he said, mysteriously, "when a thousand boys such as Eagle Feather would have been no match at all for that mouse as he used to be."

"When was that?" asked Eagle Father, looking uneasily at his sister.

"In the days of the great Dormouse," answered Iagoo. "In the days, long ago, when there were many more animals than men on the earth and the biggest of all the beasts was Dormouse. Then something strange happened—something that never happened before or since. Shall I tell you about it?"

"Oh, please do!" begged Morning Glory.

"The story I am going to tell you," began Iagoo, "is not so much a story about the dormouse as it is a story about a little boy and his sister. Yet had it not been for the dormouse, I would not be here to tell about it, and you would not be here to listen.

"To begin with, you must understand that the world in those days was a different sort of place from what it is now. Oh, yes, a different sort of place. People did not eat the flesh of animals. They lived on berries and roots and wild vegetables. The Great Spirit, who made all things on land, and in the sky and water, had not yet given men Mon-da-min, the Indian corn. There was no fire to give them heat or to cook with. In all the world there was just one small fire watched by two old witches who let nobody come near it, and until Coyote, the prairie wolf, came along and stole some of this fire, the food that people could manage to get was eaten raw, the way it grew."

"They must have been pretty hungry," said Morning Glory.

"Oh, yes, they were hungry," agreed Iagoo. "But that was not all. There were so many animals and so few people that the animals ruled the earth in their own way. The biggest of them all was Bosh-kwa-dosh, the mastodon. He was higher than the highest tree and he had an enormous appetite. But he did not stay long on earth, or there would not have been food enough even for the other animals."

"I thought you said the dormouse was the biggest," interrupted Eagle Feather.

Iagoo looked at him severely.

"At the time I speak of," he continued, "Bosh-kwa-dosh, the mastodon, had just gone away. He had not gone a bit too soon, either; for, by this time, the only people left on the whole earth were a young girl and her little brother."

"Like Eagle Feather and me?" asked Morning Glory.

"The girl was much like you," said Iagoo, patiently. "But the boy was a dwarf, who never grew to be more than three feet high. Being so much stronger and larger than her brother, she gathered all the food for both and cared for him in every way. Sometimes she would take him along with her when she went to look for berries and roots. 'He's such a very little boy,' she said to herself, 'that if I leave him all alone some big bird may swoop down and carry him off to its nest.'

"She did not know what a strange boy he was and how much mischief he could do when he set his mind upon it. One day she said to him, 'Look, little brother! I have made you a bow and some arrows. It is time you learned to take care of yourself. So when I am gone, practice shooting, for this is a thing you must know how to do.'

"Winter was coming and to keep himself from freezing the boy had nothing better than a light garment woven by his sister from the wild grasses. How could he get a warm coat? As he asked himself that question, a flock of snow birds flew down, near by, and began pecking at the fallen logs to get the worms. 'Ha!' said he, 'their feathers would make me a fine coat.' Bending his bow, he let an arrow fly. But he had not yet learned how to shoot straight. It went wide of the mark. He shot a second and a third. Then the birds took fright, and flew away.

"Each day he tried again—shooting at a tree when there was nothing better to aim at. At last he killed a snow bird, then another and another. When he had shot ten birds, he had enough. 'See, Sister,' he said, 'I shall not freeze. Now you can make me a coat from the skins of these little birds.'

"So his sister sewed the skins together and made him the coat, the first warm winter coat he had ever had. It was fine to look at and the feathers kept out the cold. Eh-yah! he was proud of it! With his bow and arrows he strutted up and down, like a little turkey cock. 'Is it true?' he asked, 'that you and I are the only persons living on earth? Perhaps if I look around I may find someone else. It will do no harm to try.'

"His sister feared he would come to some harm, but he had made up his mind to see the world for himself and off he went. But his legs were short, he was not used to walking far, and he soon grew tired. When he came to a bare place on the edge of a hill, where the sun had melted the snow, he lay down and was soon fast asleep.

"As he slept the sun played a trick on him. It was a mild winter's day. The bird skins of which the coat was made were still fresh and tender and under the full glare of the sun they began to shrivel and shrink. 'Eh-yah! What's wrong?' he muttered in his sleep, feeling the coat become tighter and tighter. Then he woke, stretched out his arms, and saw what had happened.

"The sun was nearly sinking now. The boy stood up and faced

it and shook his small fist. 'See what you have done!' he cried, with a stamp of his foot. 'You have spoiled my new birdskin coat. Never mind! You think yourself beyond my reach, up there. But I'll get my revenge on you. Just wait and see!' "

"But how could he reach the sun?" asked Morning Glory, her eyes growing rounder and rounder.

"That is what his sister asked when he told her about it," said Iagoo. "And what do you think he did? First, he did nothing at all but stretch himself out on the ground, where he lay for ten days without eating or moving. Then he turned over on the other side and lay there for ten days more. At last he rose to his feet. 'I have made up my mind,' he said. 'Sister, I have a plan to catch the sun in a noose. Find me some kind of a cord from which I can make a snare.'

"She got some tough grass and twisted it into a rope. 'That will not do,' he said. 'You must find something stronger.' He no longer talked like a little boy, but like one who was to be obeyed. Then his sister thought of her hair. She cut enough from her head to make a cord, and when she had braided it he was much pleased and said it would do. He took it from her, and drew it between his lips and as he did this it turned into a kind of metal, and grew much stronger and longer, until he had so much that he wound it around his body.

"In the middle of the night he made his way to the hill, and there he fixed a noose at the place where the sun would rise. He had to wait a long time in the cold and darkness. But at last a faint light came into the sky. As the sun rose it was caught fast in the noose and there it stayed."

Iagoo stopped talking and sat looking into the fire. One might have supposed that when he did this he saw pictures in the flames, and in the red coals, and that these pictures helped him to tell the story. But Morning Glory was impatient to hear the rest.

"Iagoo," she said, "did you forget about the dormouse?"

"Eh-yah! the dormouse! No. I have not forgotten," answered the old man, rousing himself. "When the sun did not rise as usual, the animals could not tell what had happened. Ad-ji-dau-mo, the squirrel, chattered and scolded from the branch of a pine tree. Kah-gah-gee, the raven, flapped his wings, and croaked more hoarsely than ever, to tell the others that the end of the world had come. Only Muk-wa, the bear, did not mind. He had crept into his cave for the winter and the darker it was the better he liked it.

"Wa-bun, the East Wind, was the one who brought the news. He had drawn from his quiver the silver arrows with which he chased the darkness from the valleys. But the sun had not risen to help him and the arrows fell harmless to the earth. 'Wake, wake!' he wailed. 'Someone has caught the sun in a snare. Which of all the animals will dare to cut the cord?'

"But even Coyote, the prairie wolf, who was the wisest of them all, could think of no way to free the sun. So great was the heat thrown out by its rays that he could not come within an arrow's flight of where it was caught fast in the magical noose of hair.

" 'Leave it to me!' screamed Ken-eu, the war eagle, from his nest on the cliff. 'It is I alone who soar to the sky and look the sun in the face without winking. Leave it to me!'

"Down he darted through the darkness, and up he flew again with his eagle feathers singed. Then they woke Dormouse. They had a hard time doing it, because once he went to sleep he stayed asleep for six months and it was almost impossible to arouse him. Coyote crept close to his ear and howled with all his might. It would have split the eardrum of almost any other animal. But Kug-e-been-gwa-kwa, the dormouse, only groaned and turned over on the other side and Coyote had a narrow escape from being mashed flat, like a corncake.

" 'There is only one thing that will wake him,' said Coyote, getting up and shaking himself. 'I will run to the mountain cave of

An-ne-mee-kee, the thunder. His voice is even more terrible than mine.' So off he went at a gallop.

"Soon they could hear An-ne-mee-kee coming. Boom, boom! When he shouted in the ear of Dormouse, the biggest beast on earth rose slowly to his feet. In the darkness he looked bigger than ever, almost as big as a mountain. An-ne-mee-kee, the thunder, shouted once more, to make sure that Dormouse was really wide awake and would not go to sleep again.

" 'Now,' said Coyote to Dormouse, 'it is you that will have to free the sun. If he burned one of us there would be little left but bones. But you are so big that if part of you is burned away there will still be enough. Then, in that case you would not have to eat so much, or work so hard to get it.'

"Dormouse was a stupid animal and Coyote's talk seemed true talk. Besides, as he was the biggest animal, he was expected to do the biggest things. So he made his way to the hill, where the little boy had snared the sun, and began to nibble at the noose. As he nibbled away his back got hotter and hotter. Soon it began to burn, until all the upper part of him burned away and became great heaps of ashes. At last, when he had cut through the cord with his teeth, and set the sun free, all that was left of him was an animal no larger than an ordinary mouse. What he became then, so he is today. Still, he is big enough for a mouse; and perhaps that is what Coyote really meant. Coyote, the prairie wolf, is a cunning beast, up to many tricks, and it is not always easy to tell exactly what he means."

Grasshopper

There was once a merry young Indian who could jump so high and who played so many pranks that he came to be known as Grasshopper. He was a tall, handsome fellow, always up to mischief of one kind or another. And though his tricks were sometimes amusing, he carried them much too far and so in time he came to grief.

Grasshopper owned all the things that an Indian likes most to have. In his lodge were all kinds of pipes and weapons, ermine and other choice furs, deerskin shirts wrought with porcupine quills, many pairs of beaded moccasins, and more wampum belts than one person could have honestly come by.

The truth is, Grasshopper did not get these things by his skill and courage as a hunter. He got them by shaking pieces of colored bone and wood in a wooden bowl, then throwing them on the ground. That is to say, Grasshopper was a gambler and such a lucky gambler that he easily won from others, with his game of Bowl and Counters, the things that they had obtained by risking their lives in the hunt.

If people put up with his ways, and even laughed at some of his mad pranks, it was because he could dance so well. Never had there been such a dancer. Was there a wedding to be celebrated, or some feast following a successful hunt—then who but Grasshopper could so well supply the entertainment?

He could dance with a step so light that it seemed to leave no mark upon the earth. He could dance as the Indian dances when he goes to war or when he holds a festival in honor of the corn. But the dance in which he excelled was a furious, dizzy dance, with leaps and bounds, that fairly turned the heads of the beholders.

It was then that Grasshopper became a kind of human whirlwind. As he spun round and round, his revolving body drew up the dry leaves and the dust until he all but faded from view and you saw instead what looked like a whirling cloud.

Once, when the great Manito, named Man-a-bo-zho, took a wife and came to live with the tribe, that he might teach them best how to live, Grasshopper danced at the wedding. The Beggar's Dance, he called it, and such a dance it was! On the shores of the Big-Sea-Water, Gitche Gumee, are heaps of sand rising into little hills known as dunes. Had you asked Iagoo, he would have told you that these dunes were the work of Grasshopper, who whirled the sands together and piled them into hills as he spun madly around in his dance at Man-a-bo-zho's wedding.

But though Grasshopper came to the wedding and danced this crazy Beggar's Dance, it seems probable that he did it more to please himself, and to show his skill, than to honor the great Man-a-bo-zho. Grasshopper really had no respect for anybody. When Iagoo's grandfather was in the middle of some interesting story, and had come to the most exciting part, Grasshopper likely as not would yawn and stretch himself and say in a loud whisper that he had heard it all before.

So, too, with Man-a-bo-zho. This great Manito, who was the son of the West Wind, Mud-je-kee-wis, had magic powers which he used for the good of the tribe. It was he who fasted and prayed that his people might be given food other than the wild things of the woods. And it was he whose prayer was answered with the gift of the Indian corn. Then when Kah-gah-gee, king of ravens, flew down with his band of black thieves to tear up the seed in the ground, it was Man-a-bo-zho who snared him and tied him fast to the ridge pole of his lodge, to croak out a warning to the others.

But Man-a-bo-zho's goodness and wisdom had little effect on Grasshopper. "Pooh!" he would say. "Why should an Indian bother his head with planting corn when he can draw his bow and kill a good fat deer?" Then he shook his wolfskin pouch and rattled the pieces of bone and wood. "As long as I have these," he said to himself, "I need nothing more. After all, it is everybody else that works for the man who knows how to use his head."

He walked through the village, very proud and straight, with his fan of turkey feathers, a swan's plume fastened in his long, black hair, and the tails of foxes trailing from his heels. In his white deerskin shirt, edged with ermine, his leggings and moccasins ornamented with beads and porcupine quills, he cut a fine figure. There was to be a dance that night and Grasshopper, who was a great dandy and a favorite with all the young girls and women, had decked himself out for the occasion. He had painted his face with streaks of blue and vermilion. His blue-black hair, parted in the middle and glistening with oil, hung to his shoulders in braids plaited with sweet grass. The warriors might call him Shau-go-daya, a coward, and make jokes at his expense, but he did not care. Could he not beat them all when it came to playing ball or quoits, and were not the maidens all in love with his good looks?

Meanwhile, Grasshopper wished to pass the time in some pleasant way. Glancing through the door of a lodge, he saw a group of young men seated on the ground, listening to Iagoo's stories.

"Ha!" he cried. "Have you nothing better to do? Here's a game worth playing."

He drew from his pouch the thirteen pieces of bone and wood and juggled them from one hand to the other. But no one paid any attention to him. After all, Grasshopper had "more brains in his heels than in his head." For once he had been too cunning. Fearing his skill, no one could be found who would play with him.

"Pooh!" muttered Grasshopper, as he turned away. "I see how it is. The pious Man-a-bo-zho has been preaching to them again. This village is getting to be pretty tiresome to live in. It's about time for me to strike out and find a place where the young men don't sit around and talk to the squaws."

He walked along, bent on mischief. Even the dance was forgotten. He wondered what he could do to amuse himself. As he came to the outskirts of the village, he passed the lodge of Man-a-bo-zho. "I would like to play him some trick," he said under his breath, "so he will remember me when I am gone." But he was well aware that Man-a-bo-zho was much more powerful than himself. So he hesitated, not knowing exactly what do to.

At last he walked softly to the doorway and listened, but could hear no sound of voices. "Good!" he said with a grin. "Perhaps nobody is at home." With that, he spun around the outside of the lodge, on one leg, raising a great cloud of dust. No one came out, but on the ridge pole of the lodge, the captive Kah-gah-gee, king of ravens, flapped his big black wings and screamed with a hoarse, rasping cry.

"Fool!" cried Grasshopper. "Noisy fool!"

With a bound, he leaped clear over the lodge, and then back again. And the raven screamed more harshly than ever. But within the lodge all was silent.

Grasshopper grew bolder. Going to the doorway again, he rattled the flap of buffalo hide. Nobody answered. Cautiously drawing the curtain to one side, he ventured to peer in. Then he chuckled softly. The lodge was empty.

"This is my chance!" he exclaimed. "Man-a-bo-zho is away and so is his foolish wife. I'll just pay my respects before they come back and then I'll be off for good."

Saying this, he went in and began to turn everything upside down. He threw all the bowls and kettles in a corner, filled the drinking gourds with ashes from the fire, flung the rich furs and embroidered garments this way and that, and strewed the floor with wampum belts and arrows. When he finished, one might have thought a crazy man had been there. No woman in the village was more neat and orderly than the wife of Man-a-bo-zho and Grasshopper knew this would vex her more than anything else he could do.

"Now for Man-a-bo-zho." He grinned as he left the lodge, well pleased with the mischief he had wrought.

"Caw, caw!" screamed the king of ravens.

"Kaw!" answered Grasshopper, mocking him. "A pretty sort of pet *you* are. Does Man-a-bo-zho keep you sitting there because you are so handsome? Or is it your beautiful voice?"

"With that, he made a leap to the ridge pole, seized the raven by the neck, and whirled it round and round until it was quite limp and lifeless. Then he left it hanging there, as an insult to Man-a-bo-zho.

He was now in high good humor and went his way through the forest, whistling and singing and turning handsprings to amuse the squirrels. There was a high rock, overlooking the lake, from the top of which one could view the country for miles and miles. Grasshopper climbed it. He could see the village plainly so he thought he would wait there until Man-a-bo-zho came home. That would be part of the joke.

As he sat there many birds darted around him, flying close over his head. Man-a-bo-zho called these fowls of the air his chickens and he had put them under his protection. But Grasshopper grew reckless. Along came a flock of the mountain chickens and he strung his bow and shot them as they flew, for no better reason than because they were Man-a-bo-zho's and not because he needed them for food. Bird after bird fell, pierced by his arrows. When they had fallen, he would throw their bodies down the cliff, upon the beach below.

At last Kay-oshk, the seagull, spied him at this cruel sport and gave the alarm. "Grasshopper is killing us," he called. "Fly, brothers! Fly away and tell our protector that Grasshopper is slaying us with his arrows."

When Man-a-bo-zho heard the news, his eyes flashed fire, and he spoke in a voice of thunder: "Grasshopper must die for this! He cannot escape me. Though he fly to the ends of the earth, I shall follow and visit my vengeance upon him."

On his feet he bound his magic moccasins with which, at each stride, he could step a full mile. On his hands he drew his magic mittens with which, at one blow, he could shatter the hardest rock. Then he started in pursuit.

Grasshopper had heard the warning call of the seagull and knew it was time to be off. He, too, could run. So fleet of foot was he that he could shoot an arrow ahead of him and reach the spot where it fell before it dropped to earth. He also had the power to change himself into other shapes and it was almost impossible to kill him. If, for example, he entered the body of a beaver and the beaver was slain, no sooner had its flesh grown cold than the *Fee-bi,* or spirit, of Grasshopper would leave the dead body and Grasshopper would become a man again, ready for some new adventure.

But at first he trusted to his legs and to his cunning. On rushed Man-a-bo-zho, breathing vengeance. Swiftly, like a moving shadow, fled Grasshopper. Through the forest and across the hills he fled, faster than the hare. His pursuer was hot on the trail. Once he came upon the forest bed where the grass was still warm and bent, but Grasshopper, who had rested there, was far away. Once Man-a-bo-zho, high on a mountain, spied him in the meadow below. Grasshopper had shown himself on purpose and mocked the great Manito and defied him. The truth is, Grasshopper was just a bit conceited.

At last he grew tired of running. Not that his leg ached him or his feet were sore. But this kind of life was not much to his liking, and he kept his eye open for something new. Pretty soon he came to a stream where the water was backed by a dam, so that it flooded the banks. Grasshopper had run about a thousand miles that day— counting all the turns and twists. He was hot and dusty and the pond, with its waterlilies and rushes, looked cool and refreshing. From far, far away came a faint sound. It was the voice of Man-a-bo-zho, shouting his war cry.

"Tiresome fellow!" said Grasshopper. "I could almost wish I were a beaver and lived down there at the bottom of the pond where no one would disturb me."

Then up popped the head of a beaver, who looked at Grasshopper suspiciously.

"Don't be alarmed. I left my bow and arrows over there in the grass," explained Grasshopper. "Besides, I was just thinking I would like to be a beaver myself. What do you say to that?"

"I shall have to consult Ahmeek, our chief," answered the friendly animal.

Down he dived to the bottom. Pretty soon Ahmeek's head appeared above the water, followed by the heads of twenty other beavers.

"Let me be one of you," said Grasshopper. "You have a pleasant home down there in the clear, cool water and I am tired of the life I lead."

Ahmeek was pleased that such a strong, handsome young Indian should wish to join their company.

"But I can help you," he answered, "only after you have plunged into the pond. Do you think you can change yourself into one of us?"

"That is easy," said Grasshopper.

He waded into the water up to his waist and behold! he had a broad flat tail. Deeper and deeper he went. As the water closed above his head he became a beaver, with glossy, black fur and feet webbed like a duck's. Down he sank with the others to the bottom, which was covered with heaps of logs and branches.

"That," explained Ahmeek, "is the food we have stored for the winter. We eat the bark and you will soon be as fat as any of us."

"But I want to be even fatter," said Grasshopper. "Fatter and ten times as big."

"As you please," agreed Ahmeek. "We can help to make you just as big as you wish."

They reached the lodge where the beavers lived and entered the doorway, leading into a number of large rooms. Grasshopper selected the largest one for himself.

"Now," he said, "bring me all the food I can eat and when I am big enough I will be your chief."

The beavers were willing. They set to work getting quantities of the juiciest bark for Grasshopper, who was delighted with this lazy life and did little more than eat or sleep. Bigger and bigger he grew, until at last he was ten times the size of Ahmeek and could barely manage to move around in his lodge. He was perfectly happy.

But one day the beaver who kept watch up above, among the rushes of the pond, came swimming to the lodge in a state of great excitement.

"The hunters are after us," he panted. "It is indeed Man-a-bo-zho himself, with his hunters. They are breaking down our dam!"

Even as he spoke, the water in the pond sank lower and lower. The next moment came the tramping of feet, as the hunters leaped upon the roof of the lodge, trying to break it open.

All the beavers but Grasshopper scampered out of the lodge and escaped into the stream, where they hid themselves in deep pools or swam far down with the current. Grasshopper did his best to follow them, but could not. The doorway was too small for his big, fat body. When he tried to go through he found himself stuck fast.

Then the roof gave way and the head of an Indian appeared.

"Ty-au!" he called. *"Tut-ty-au!* See what's here! This must be Me-shau-mik, the king of the beavers."

Man-a-bo-zho came and gave one look.

"It's Grasshopper!" he cried. "I can see through his tricks. It's Grasshopper in the skin of a beaver."

Then they fell upon him with their clubs. And eight tall Indians, having swung his limp carcass upon poles, carried it off in triumph through the woods.

But his *Fee-bi,* or spirit, was still in the body of the beaver and struggled to escape. The Indians bore him to their lodges and prepared to make a feast. Then, when the squaws were ready to skin him, his flesh was quite cold and the spirit of Grasshopper left the beaver's body and glided swiftly away. As the shadowy shape fled across the prairie, into the forest, the watchful Man-a-bo-zho saw it take the human form of Grasshopper and he started in pursuit.

Grasshopper's life among the beavers had made him lazier than ever and as he ran he looked around for some easier way than running. Soon he came upon a herd of elk, a species of deer with large, spreading horns. The elk were feeding contentedly and looked sleek and fat.

"They lead a free and happy life," said Grasshopper as he watched them. "Why fatigue myself with running? I'll change myself into an elk and join their band."

Horns sprouted from his head. In a few minutes the transformation was complete. Still he was not satisfied.

"I am hardly big enough," he said to the leader. "My feet are much too small and my horns should be twice the size of yours. Is there nothing I can do to make them grow?"

"Yes," answered the leader of the elks. "But you do it at your own risk."

He took Grasshopper into the woods and showed him a bright red berry that hung in clusters on some small, low bushes.

"Eat these," he said, "and nothing else and your horns and feet will soon be much bigger than ours. However, it would be wise if you did not eat too many of them."

The berries were delicious. Grasshopper felt that he could not get enough and he ate them greedily whenever he could find them. Before long his feet had grown so large and heavy he could hardly keep up with the herd, while his horns had such a huge spread that he sometimes found them rather in his way.

One cold day the herd went into the woods for shelter. Pretty soon some of the elks who had lingered behind came rushing by with snorts of alarm. Hunters were pursuing them.

"Run!" called out the leader to Grasshopper. "Follow us out on the prairie where the Indians cannot catch us."

Grasshopper tried to follow them, but his big feet weighed him down and he ran slowly. Then, as he plunged madly through a thicket, his spreading horns became entangled in some low branches that held him fast. Already several arrows had whizzed by him. Another pierced his heart and he sank to the ground.

Along came the hunters with a whoop. *"Ty-au!"* they exclaimed when they saw the enormous elk. "It is he who made the large tracks on the prairie. *Ty-au!"*

As they were skinning him, Man-a-boo-zho joined the party. And at that moment the *Fee-bi,* or spirit, of Grasshopper escaped through the mouth of the dead elk and passed swiftly to the open plains, like a puff of white smoke driven before the wind. Then, as Man-a-bo-zho watched it melt away he saw once more the mortal shape of Grasshopper. And once more he followed after, breathing vengeance.

As Grasshopper ran on, a new thought came into his head.

Above him in the clear blue sky the birds wheeled and soared. "There is the place for me," he said, "far up in the sky. Let me have wings and I can laugh at Man-a-bo-zho."

Ahead of him was a lake. Approaching it he saw a flock of wild geese known as as brant, feeding among the rushes. "Ha," said Grasshopper, admiring them as they sailed smoothly here and there. "They will soon be winging their way to the North. I would like to fly in their company."

He spoke to them, calling them Pish-ne-kuh, his brothers, and they consented to receive him as one of the flock. So he floated on his back until feathers sprouted on him and he became a brant, with a broad black beak and a tail that would guide him through the air as a rudder steers a ship.

Greedy as ever, he fed long after the others had had enough so that he soon grew into the biggest brant ever seen. His beak looked like the paddles of a canoe. When he spread his wings they were as large as two large *au-puk-wa,* or mats. The wild geese gazed at him in astonishment. "You must fly in the lead," they said.

"No," answered Grasshopper. "I would rather fly behind."

"As you please," they told him. "But you will have to be careful. By all means keep your head and neck straight out before you, and do not look down as you fly or you may meet with an accident."

It was a beautiful sight to see them flap their wings, stretch their long necks, and rise with a "whir" from the lake, mounting the wind and rushing on before it. They flew with a breeze from the south, faster and faster, until their speed was like the flight of an arrow.

One day, passing over a village, they could hear the people shouting. The Indians were amazed at the size of the big brant flying in the rear of the flock. They were yelling as loud as they could yell and their cries made Grasshopper curious. One voice especially seemed familiar to him and he could not resist the temptation to draw in his neck and stretch it down toward the earth. As he did so, the strong wind caught his tail and turned him over and over. In vain he tried to recover his balance. The wind whirled him round and round, as it whirls a leaf. The earth came nearer and the shouts of the Indians grew louder in his ears. At last he fell with a thud and lay lifeless.

It was a fine feast of wild goose that had dropped so suddenly from the skies. The hungry Indians pounced upon him and began to pluck his feathers. This was the very village where Grasshopper had once lived. Little had he dreamed that he would ever return to supply it with such a dinner, a dinner at which he himself was to be the best dish.

But again his *Fee-bi,* or spirit, went forth, and fled in the form of Grasshopper. Again Man-a-bo-zho, shouting his war cry, followed after.

Grasshopper had now come to the desert places where there were few trees and no signs of animal life: Man-a-bo-zho was gaining on him. He must play some new trick. Coming at last to a tall pine tree growing in the rock, he climbed it, pulled off all the green needles, and scattered them about, leaving the branches quite bare. Then he took to his heels again. When Man-a-bo-zho came the pine spoke to him, saying, "See what Grasshopper has done. Without my foliage I am sure to die. Great Manito, I pray you give me back my green dress."

Man-a-bo-zho, who loves and protects all trees, had pity on the pine. He collected the scattered needles and restored them to the branches. Then he hastened on with such speed that he overtook Grasshopper and put his hand out to clutch him. But Grasshopper stepped quickly aside and spun round and round on one leg in his whirlwind dance, until the air all about was filled with leaves and sand. In the midst of this whirlwind he sprang into a hollow tree and changed himself into a snake. Then he crept out through the roots, and not a moment too soon. For Man-a-bo-zho smote the tree with one of his magic mittens and crumbled it to powder.

Grasshopper changed himself back into his human form and ran for dear life. The only thing left for him to do was to hide. But where? In his headlong flight he had come again to the shores of the Great Lake. He saw rising before him the high cliff of the Picture Rocks. If he could but manage to reach these rocks, the Manito of the Mountain, who lived in one of the gloomy caverns, might let him in. Sure enough! As he reached the cliff, calling out for help, the Manito opened the door and told him to enter.

Hardly had the big door closed with a bang, than along came Man-a-bo-zho. With his mitten he gave a tap on the rock that made the splinters fly.

"Open!" he cried in a terrible voice.

But the Manito was brave and hospitable.

"I have sheltered you," he said to Grasshopper, "and I would rather die myself than give you up."

Man-a-bo-zho waited, but no answer came.

"As you will," he said at last. "If the door is not opened to me by night, I shall call upon the thunder and the lightning to do my bidding."

The hours passed. Darkness fell. Then from a black cloud that had gathered over the Great Lake, Way-wass-i-mo, the red-eyed lightning, shot his bolts of fire. Crash—boom—crash! An-ne-mee-kee, the thunder, shouted hoarsely from the heavens. A wild wind arose. The trees of the forest swayed and groaned. The foxes hid in their holes.

Way-wass-i-mo, the lightning, leaped from the black cloud and darted at the cliff. The rock trembled. The door was shattered and fell apart. Out from his gloomy cavern came the Manito of the Mountain, asking Man-a-bo-zho for mercy. It was granted and the Manito fled to the hills.

Grasshopper then appeared. The next moment he was buried

under a mass of rock shaken loose by An-ne-mee-kee, the thunder. This time he had been killed in his human form. He could play his mad pranks no more.

But Man-a-bo-zho, the merciful, remembered that Grasshopper was not wholly bad.

"Your *Fee-bi,*" he said, "must no longer remain upon the earth in any form whatever. As a man you lived a idle, foolish life and you are no longer wanted here. Instead, I shall permit you to inhabit the skies."

Saying this, he took the ghost of Grasshopper and clothed it in the shape of the war eagle, bidding him to be chief of all the fowls.

But Grasshopper, the mischievous, is not forgotten by the people. In the late winter days, snow fine as powder fills the air like a vapor. It keeps the hunger from his traps, the fisherman from his hole in the ice. Suddenly a puff of wind seizes this light, powdery snow, blows it round and round, and sets it whirling along. And when this happens, the Indians laugh and say, "Look! There goes Grasshopper. See how well he dances."

Mish-o-sha, the Magician

n the heart of the great green forest there once lived a hunter whose lodge was many miles distant from the wigwams of his tribe. His wife had long since died, and he dwelt there all alone with his two young sons, who grew up as best they could without a mother's care. When the father was away on a hunting trip the boys had no companions but the birds and beasts of the forest and with some of the smaller animals they became fast friends. Ad-ji-dau-mo, the squirrel, scampering from tree to tree, would let his nutshells fall on the roof of the lodge. That was his way of knocking at the door, coming to pay a morning call. He was a great talker, without much to say—as is often so with those whose voices are seldom still. But he was bright and merry, chattering away cheerfully about nothing in particular. And it made no difference whether you listened to him or not.

Wa-bo-se, the little white hare, was another friend. One winter's day, when forest food was scarce, O-ne-o-ta, the lynx, was just about to pounce upon him when the boys' father let fly an arrow— and O-ne-o-ta was no longer interested in little white hares. Wa-bo-se was grateful for this and sometimes, in his shy way, he tried to show it.

The father and the boys lived mostly on big game, like bear and venison. This meat would be cut in strips and cured. Sometimes it had to last them many a long day, when game was scarce or the woods so dry for want of rain that the twigs would snap under the hunter's feet and warn the animals he was coming. So the boys were used to being left alone for weeks at a time when their father was absent.

Then came a season of famine. No berries grew on the bushes, grass withered on the stalk, few acorns hung on the oaks. Some of the brooks went dry. Thus it happened that the hunter had gone far in search of game.

Many months passed. When Seegwun, the elder boy, saw that but little meat remained, he said to his younger brother, Ioscoda, "Let us take what meat is left and strike out through the forest, toward the north. I remember our father saying that many moons distant lies a great lake called Gitche Gumee whose waters are alive with fish."

"But can we find our way?" asked Ioscoda, doubtfully.

"Never fear!" called out a voice from overhead.

It was Ad-ji-dau-mo, the squirrel, frisky as ever, though a little lean for lack of nuts.

"I'll go along with you," he continued, "and so will Wa-bo-se, the white hare. He can hop ahead and find the trail and I can jump from tree to tree and keep a lookout. Between us, we are bound to go right."

It proved to be a good idea and Wa-bo-se took the lead. Where the tail was overgrown with grass he would nose his way along the ground, without once going wrong. Where the track was over a plain he would run ahead, then stop and sit up on his haunches to wait for the boys, his long ears pricked up and moving to detect the slightest danger.

But nothing happened to alarm them. The lynx, the wild cat, and the wolf had all fled before the famine and the silent forest was empty of savage beasts. On and on they went, until it seemed as if the woods would never end. Then, one day, Ad-ji-dau-mo climbed a tall pine, from whose topmost bough he could see far over the forest. The sun was shining bright. As he cocked his eye and looked toward the north something that seemed to meet the sky sparkled like silver. It was Gitche Gumee, the Great Lake.

They had reached a place where nuts were plentiful and many green things grew that would fatten the white hare. So Wa-bo-se and the squirrel bade good-bye to the boys, who could now make their way with ease. Soon they came to the edge of the woods. They heard a piping cry. It was Twee-tweesh-ke-way, the plover, flying along the beach. In another moment the great glittering waters lay before them.

Seegwun with his sharp hunting knife, cut a limb from an ash tree and made a bow. From an oak bough he whittled some arrows, which he tipped with flint. He found feathers fallen from a gull's wing for the shaft. A strip cut from his deerskin shirt supplied the bowstring. Then giving the bow and arrow to Ioscoda to practice with, he gathered some seed pods from the wild rose, to stay their hunger.

An arrow, badly aimed by his brother, fell into the lake and Seegwun waded in to recover it. He had walked into the water until it reached his waist and put out his hand to grasp the arrow, when suddenly, as if by magic, a canoe came skimming along like a bird. In the canoe was an ugly old man who reached out, seized the astonished boy and pulled him on board.

"If I must go with you take my brother, too!" begged Seegwun. "If he is left here, all alone, he will starve."

But Mish-o-sha, the magician, only laughed. Then striking the side of the canoe with his hand and uttering the magic words *Chemaun Poll,* it shot across the lake like a thing alive, so that the beach was quickly lost to sight. Soon the canoe came to rest on a sandy shore and Mish-o-sha, leaping out, beckoned Seegwun to follow.

They had landed on an island. Before them, in a grove of cedars, were two wigwams, or lodges. From the smaller one two lovely young girls came out and stood looking at them.

To Seegwun, who had never before seen a girl, these maidens looked like spirits from the skies. He gazed at them in wonder, half expecting they would vanish. For their part they looked at him without smiling. In their dark eyes were only sympathy and sadness.

"My daughters!" said the old man to Seegwun, with a chuckle that displayed his long, yellow teeth. Then turning to the girls he asked, "Are you not glad to see me safely back? And are you not pleased with my handsome young friend here?"

They bent their heads politely, but said nothing.

"It's a long time since you were favored with such a visitor," he went on in a loud whisper to the elder girl. "He would make you a fine husband."

The maiden murmured something under her breath and Mish-o-sha gave her a wicked look.

"We shall see, we shall see!" he muttered to himself, laughing like a magpie and rubbing his long, bony hands together.

Seegwun, much troubled in mind and hardly knowing what to make of it all, resolved to keep his eyes open. Luckily Mish-o-sha was sometimes careless. He walked on ahead and entered his lodge, leaving the others together. Whereupon the elder girl, approaching Seegwun, spoke to him quickly.

"We are not his daughters," she said. "He brought us here as he brought you. He hates the human race. Every moon he seizes a young man and pretends he has borne him here as a husband for me. But soon he takes him off in his canoe and the young man never comes back. We feel sure Mish-o-sha has made away with them all."

"What must I do?" asked Seegwun. "I care less for myself than for my little brother. He was left behind on a wild beach and may die of hunger."

"Ah!" said the maiden. "You are really good and unselfish. No matter what comes of it we must aid you. Ko-ko-ko-ho, the great owl, keeps watch all night on the bare limb of that big cedar. Wait until Mish-o-sha falls asleep, then wrap yourself from head to foot in his blanket and steal softly to the door of our lodge. Whisper my name, Nin-i-mo-sha, and I shall come out and tell you what to do."

"Nin-i-mo-sha," murmured the youth. "What a beautiful name!" Then, before he could thank her, the girls were gone.

Mish-o-sha now appeared and made a sign to Seegwun to join him. The old man seemed to be in a good humor and passed the time telling stories, but Seegwun was not deceived by this pretense of friendship. When the magician was sound asleep, he rose, wrapped Mish-o-sha's blanket around him, and walked carefully to the door of the little lodge.

"Nin-i-mo-sha!" he whispered and his heart beat fast; for Nin-i-mo-sha in the Indian tongue means "My Sweetheart."

"Seegwun!" she answered, and his name, meaning "Spring," came like music from her lips.

She drew aside the curtain, and came out. "Here," she said, "is food that will last your brother for several days. Get into Mish-o-sha's canoe, pronounce the magic charm, and it will take you where you wish. You can be back before daybreak."

"But the owl?" asked Seegwun. "Will he not cry out?"

"Walk with a stoop, the way Mish-o-sha walks," she explained. "Ko-ko-ko-ho, when he sees you, will cry 'Hoot, hoot!' You must answer, 'Hoot, hoot, whoo! Mish-o-sha.' Then he will let you pass."

Seegwun did as he was told and was soon skimming across the lake. Having landed on the beach he began to bark like a squirrel. At this friendly signal his brother ran up and flung his arms around him. Seegwun made a shelter for the boy and told him he would come again. Then he returned in the canoe and was soon fast asleep in the magician's lodge.

Mish-o-sha, who trusted in his owl, suspected nothing. How should he know what lovers can do when they put their heads together?

"You have slept well, my son," said he. "And now we have a pleasant journey before us. We are going to an island where thousands of gulls lay their eggs in the sand and we shall get all we can carry away."

Remembering what Nin-i-mo-sha had said Seegwun shivered. But she kissed her hand and waved him a good-bye. And this put heart in him.

As the canoe sped away he made sure that his hunting knife slipped easily in its sheath. And he did not take his eyes off Mish-o-sha for a moment.

When they reached the island the gulls rose in great numbers and flew screaming above their heads.

"You gather the eggs," said the magician, "while I keep watch in the canoe."

Seegwun hastened ashore, glad to leave the old man's company. Then the magician cried out to the gulls, "Ho, my feathered friends! Here is the human offering I promised you when you agreed to call me master. Fly down, my pretty ones! Fly down, and devour him!"

Striking the side of his canoe, he abandoned the youth to the mercy of the birds.

With harsh cries the gulls swept down on Seegwun. Never had he heard such a clamor. Ten thousand wings beat the air and stirred it like a storm. Whirling and darting they came upon him in a

cloud. But Seegwun did not flinch. Shouting the *Saw-saw-quan,* or war cry, he seized the first bird that attacked him. Then, grasping it by the neck, he held it high above his head in his left hand and with his right hand drew his knife, which glittered in the sun.

"Stop!" he cried. "Stop, you poor fools! Beware the vengeance of the Great Spirit."

The gulls paused in their attack, but still circled around him, with sharp beaks extended.

"Hear me, O gulls!" he continued. "The Great Spirit gave you life that you might serve mankind. Slay me and you slay one made to rule over all the beasts and birds. I tell you, beware!"

"But Mish-o-sha is all powerful," screamed the gulls. "He has bidden us destroy you."

"Mish-o-sha is no Manito," answered Seegwun. "He is only a wicked magician who would use you for his own evil ends. Bear me on your wings back to his island, for it is he who must be destroyed."

Then the gulls, persuaded that Mish-o-sha had tricked them, drew close together that the youth might lie upon their backs. Rising on the wind they carried him across the waters, setting him down gently by the lodge before the magician had arrived there.

Nin-i-mo-sha rejoiced when she saw it was really Seegwun. "I was not mistaken in you," she told him. "It is plain that the Great Spirit protects you. But Mish-o-sha will try again, so be on your guard."

The magician now arrived in his magic canoe. When he saw Seegwun he tried to smile pleasantly. But having had little practice in thinking kind thoughts, he only grinned like a gargoyle, which, excepting perhaps the hyena, has the most painful possible smile.

"Good, my son!" he managed to say. "You must not misunderstand me. I did it to test your courage. And now Nin-i-mo-sha is sure to love you. Ah, my children, you will make a happy pair!"

Nin-i-mo-sha turned away to hide her disgust, but Seegwun pretended to believe the malicious old man was in earnest.

"However," continued the magician, "I owe you something for having seemed to play you such a trick. I see you wear no ornaments. Come with me to the Island of Glittering Shells and soon you will be attired as becomes a handsome warrior."

The island where they landed was indeed a wonderful place, covered with colored shells that gleamed in the sun like jewels.

"Look!" said Mish-o-sha, as they walked along the beach. "Out here a little way. See it shining on the bottom."

Seegwun waded in. When the water reached his thighs, the magician made a leap for the canoe and shoved it far out into the lake.

"Come, King of Fishes!" he called. "You have always served me well. Here is your reward."

Then, striking his canoe, he quickly disappeared.

Immediately an enormous fish, with jaws wide open, rose to the surface a few feet away. But Seegwun only smiled, saying as he drew his long blade, "Know, monster, that I am Seegwun—named after him whose breath warms the icebound waters and clothes the hills with green. The cowardly Mish-o-sha, fearing the anger of the Great Spirit, seeks to make you do what he dares not do himself. Spill but one drop of my blood and it will dye the waters of the lake in which all your tribe will miserably perish."

"Mish-o-sha has deceived me," said the King of Fishes. "He promised me a tender maiden and has brought instead a youth with the eyes of a warrior. How shall I aid you, my Master?"

"Wretch!" exclaimed Seegwun. "Rejoice that he did not keep his frightful promise. You deserve to die at my hands, but I will give you a chance to repent. Take me on your back to the island of Mish-o-sha, and I will spare your life."

The King of Fishes hastened to take Seegwun astride his broad back and swam so swiftly that he reached the island soon after

Mish-o-sha. The magician was explaining to Nin-i-mo-sha how the youth had fallen from the canoe into the jaws of a big fish, when along came Seegwun himself, strolling up from the lake as if he had returned from an everyday excursion. Even so, Mish-o-sha still sought to excuse himself.

"My daughter," said he. "I was only trying to find out how much you cared for him."

But all the while he was saying to himself that the next time he would not fail. And the next time was the very next day.

"My owl is growing old and cannot live much longer," he explained. "I should like to catch a young eagle and tame him. Will you help me?"

Seegwun consented and went with him in the magic canoe to a rocky point of land reaching out into the lake. There, in the fork of a tall pine, was an eagle's nest, in which were some young eagles who could not yet fly.

"Quick!" said Mish-o-sha. "Climb the tree before the old birds return."

Seegwun had almost reached the nest when the magician spoke to the pine, commanding it to grow taller. At once it began to rise until it was so high, and swayed so in the wind, that he felt it would take all his courage to get down again. At the same time the magician uttered a peculiar cry, at which the father and mother eagles came swooping from the clouds to protect their young.

"Ho, ho!" laughed Mish-o-sha. "This time I have made no mistake. Either you will fall and break your neck or the eagles will scratch your eyes out."

Striking his canoe he vanished in the mist.

The eagles now circled around Seegwun, who, resting on a branch, thus addressed them: "My brothers, behold the eagle's feather in my hair! It proves my admiration for your bravery and skill. Yet in me you see your master. For I am a man and you are only birds. Obey me, then, and bear me to Mish-o-sha's island."

This praise pleased the eagles, who respected the youth's cool courage. Mounting on the back of the enormous male bird, Seegwun was borne through the air and set down safely on the enchanted island.

Mish-o-sha now saw that neither bird nor beast would harm this handsome youth, who seemed to be protected by some powerful Manito. It must be done some other way.

"One more test," he said to Seegwun, "and then you may take Nin-i-mo-sha for your wife. But first you must prove your skill as a hunter. Come!"

They made a lodge in the forest. Mish-o-sha, by his magic, caused a snowstorm, with a stinging gale from the north like a flight of icy arrows. Seegwun, that night, before going to sleep, had hung his moccasins and leggings by the fire to dry. Mish-o-sha, rising first, at daybreak, took one of each and threw them into the flames. Then he rubbed his hands and laughed like a prairie wolf.

"What is it?" asked Seegwun, sitting up.

"Alas, my son!" said Mish-o-sha. "I was just too late. This is the season of the moon when fire attracts all things. It has drawn to it one of your moccasins and leggings and destroyed them. *Yeo, yeo!* I should have warned you."

Seegwun held his tongue, although the situation was plain enough. Mish-o-sha meant that he should freeze to death. But Seegwun, praying silently to his Manito for aid, took from the fireplace a charred stick with which he blackened one leg and foot, murmuring a charm at the same time. Then, putting on his remaining moccasin and legging, he was ready for the hunt.

Their way led through snow and ice into thickets of thorn, and over bogs half-frozen, where Seegwun sank to the knees. But his prayer had been heard. The charm worked and the youth walked on, dry shod. With his first arrow he slew a bear.

"Now," he said, looking the magician full in the eye. "I see you are suffering from the cold. Let us go back to your island."

At Seegwun's bold look, Mish-o-sha bent his head and mumbled some foolish answer. At last he had met his match, and he knew it.

"Take the bear on your shoulders!" commanded Seegwun. Again the magician obeyed.

For the first time they returned together to the island, where the two young girls looked on in amazement to see the proud Mish-o-sha staggering under the weight of the bear, grunting with helpless rage.

"His power is broken," agreed Nin-i-mo-sha when Seegwun had told her all. "But we shall never sleep in safety until we are really rid of him. What is best to do?"

They put their heads together and when they had talked it over, Nin-i-mo-sha laughed merrily. "He deserves a greater punishment," she said. "The world will not be safe as long as he has life. Yet what we plan to do will revenge us, without shedding a single drop of blood."

The next day Seegwun said to the magician, "It is time that we rescued my brother, whom we left all alone on the beach. Come with me."

Mish-o-sha made a wry face, but prepared to go. Landing on the beach, they soon spied the boy, who joyfully clambered into the canoe. Then Seegwun said to the old man, "Those red willows over on the bank would make good smoking mixture. Could you manage to climb up there and cut me some?"

"To be sure, my son, to be sure," answered Mish-o-sha, walking rapidly toward the willows. "I am not so weak and good-for-nothing as you seem to think."

Seegwun struck the canoe with his hand, pronouncing the magic words, *Chemaun Poll*. And away it went with the two brothers aboard, leaving the magician high and dry and gnashing his yellow teeth.

The girls ran to meet them at the shore, Nin-i-mo-sha rejoicing that the old man had been left behind while her sister could think of nothing but the attractive boy who looked so much like his big brother.

"But Mish-o-sha can call the canoe back to him," said Nin-i-mo-sha, "until a way is found to break the charm. Someone must keep watch, with his hand upon it."

Ioscoda begged permission to do his part, so they left him with night coming on, sitting on the sand and holding fast to the canoe.

It was a tiresome task for a young boy already weary with long waiting. To amuse himself he began to count the stars. First he counted those in the Big Dipper and the Little Dipper, then the ones that look like a high-back chair, and the three big bright ones in the belt of Orion the Hunter. He did not know them by these names, which were given them long afterward. But he recognized the cluster called O-jeeg An-nung, the Fisher, who brought Summer from the sky because his boy was cold.

Ioscoda was also cold, sitting there in the wet sand. But Indian boys do not complain. Yet seeing the Fisher stars he thought of his own dear father and wondered where he might be. He did not cry, but he found himself looking at the sky through a kind of fog. What was it? He rubbed his eyes, lost his count, and began all over again.

The boy could reckon only with his fingers and his toes, and Ioscoa's toes were tucked away snugly in his moccasins, quite out of sight and question. How many fingers had he counted—and how—many—stars—?

The fog, or whatever it was, filled his eyes. "Lap, lap!" went the little waves, rocking the canoe like a cradle. "Soo, soo!" sighed the wind in the cedars. All else that was earthly nodded and was still. Even the stars blinked and winked, as if weary of watching the world.

And Ioscoda slept.

"Whoo, whoo!" the cry of Ko-ko-ko-ho, the owl, shrilled evilly on the ears. It was only for a moment. The shadows lifted, a squirrel barked. Wa-bun, the East Wind, rising above the rim of the waters, let loose his silver arrows. It was day.

Ioscoda sat up, only half aroused, and looked over the lake. Was he still on the wild beach, waiting for his brother? Then he remembered and gave a guilty start. The canoe was gone!

Gone, but come again! There it appeared, gliding straight toward him. And in it sat Mish-o-sha.

"Good morning, child!" called the magician, as the canoe grated on the sand, "Are you not glad to see your grandfather again?"

Ioscoda clenched his small fists. He was very brave and he was angry.

"You are *not* my grandfather," he said, "and I am *not* glad to see you again."

"*Esa, esa!* Shame, shame!" chuckled the old man. "But Seegwun will be glad to see me and so will my dear daughters. I hope they have not worried about me."

He was much pleased with his cleverness in outwitting them all and was now as impudent as before. But Seegwun bided his time. He thought of another plan.

"Grandfather," said he, "it seems that we must continue to live here together. Let us therefore lay in a supply of meat for the winter. Come with me to the mainland. I am sure you must be a mighty hunter."

Mish-o-sha's vanity was his weakest point. "*Eh, yah!*" he answered boastfully. "I can run all day with a dead deer on my back. I have done it."

"Good!" said Seegwun. "The wind is going north again, and we shall need all our strength on the march."

Now Seegwun had somehow learned the magician's dearest secret, which was this: Mish-o-sha's left leg and foot were the only parts of his body that could be harmed. No arrow could pierce his heart. A war club brought down upon his head would be shattered into splinters. As well strike him with a straw. But his left leg and foot. Ah! It was not for rheumatism that his legging was so well laced. And *why* did he always sit down with his left foot tucked up under him? Ha! Why, indeed? Seegwun had found the answer.

They made a rude lodge in the forest, just as they had done before. And again it came bitter cold. Only this time it was Seegwun who brought the storm. He could not help laughing. There was the blazing fire and there on the couch was Mish-o-sha, sound asleep.

Seegwun softly rose, took both the magician's moccasins and leggings and threw them into the flames.

"Get up, Grandfather," he called. "It's the season when fire attracts all things and I fear you have lost something you may need."

When Mish-o-sha saw what had happened he looked so frightened that Seegwun was almost sorry for him. But remembering Nin-i-mo-sha and his little brother, he could think of no other way. "We must be going," he said.

They set out through the snow. My, how cold it was! Mish-o-sha began to run, thinking this would help; while Seegwun followed, fearing that if he led, the magician might send an arrow through his back. After running for an hour, the magician was quite out of breath and his legs and feet were growing numb and stiff.

They had come to the edge of the forest and reached the shore of the lake. Here Mish-o-sha stopped. When he tried to take another step he could not lift his feet. How heavy they had grown! He tried again, but something strange had happened. His toes sank into the sand and took the form of roots. The feathers in his hair, and then the hair itself, changed gradually into leaves. His outstretched arms were branches, swaying in the wind. Bark appeared on his body.

Seegwun looked and wondered. That which had been Mish-o-sha was no longer a man, but a tree, a sycamore hung with button balls, leaning crookedly toward the lake.

At last the wicked old magician had met his master. No more would his evil spell be cast on the young and innocent. Seegwun lingered a moment, to make sure that Mish-o-sha would not come to life. Then he took his way across the water, where the others, anxiously awaiting him, were told the good news.

"Mish-o-sha is no more," said Seegwun. "He can never harm us again. Let us leave this place where we have suffered so much and make our home on the mainland."

So together they went forth, his sweetheart, her sister, and the boy, with Seegwun showing the way. The trail he took led them again to the great forest and once more to the ledge from which he had set out. And there they lived happily for the rest of their days.

The Fairy Bride

nce there was a lovely girl named Neen-i-zu, the only daughter of an Indian chief, who lived on the shore of Lake Superior. Neen-i-zu, in the Indian language, means "My Dear Life." It was plain that her parents loved her tenderly and did everything in their power to make her happy and to shield her from any possible harm.

There was but one thing that made them uneasy. Neen-i-zu was a favorite with the other young girls of the village and joined them in their play. But she liked best of all to walk by herself in the forest or to follow some dim trail that led to the heart of the little hills. Sometimes she would be absent for many hours and when she returned her eyes had the look of one who has dwelt in secret places and seen things strange and mysterious. Nowadays, some persons would have called Neen-i-zu "romantic." Others, who can never see a thing that is not just beneath their noses, would have laughed a little, in a superior sort of way, and said she was a "dreamer."

What was it that Neen-i-zu saw and heard during these lonely walks in the secret places of the hills? Was it perhaps the fairies? She did not say. But her mother, who wished her to be more like other girls and who would have liked to see her marry and settle down, was much disturbed.

The mischievous little fairies known as Puk-Wudjies were believed to inhabit the sand dunes where Neen-i-zu so often went to walk. These were the sand hills made by Grasshopper when he danced so madly at Man a bo zho's wedding, whirling the sand into great drifts and mounds that may be seen to this very day. The Puk-Wudjies loved these hills, which were seldom visited by the Indians. It was just the place for leapfrog and all-hands-'round. In the twilight of summer days they were said to gather here in little bands, playing all manner of pranks. Then, as night came, they would make haste to hide themselves in a grove of pine trees known as the *Manito Wac,* or the Wood of the Spirits.

No one had ever come close to them, but fishermen, paddling their canoes on the lake, had caught glimpses of them from afar and had heard the tiny voices of these merry little men as they laughed and called to one another. When the fishermen tried to follow, the Puk-Wudjies would vanish in the woods, but their footprints, no larger than a child's, could be seen on the damp sand of a little lake in the hills.

If anything more were needed to convince those doubters who did not believe in fairies, the proof was quickly supplied by fishermen and hunters who were victims of their tricks. The Puk-Wudjies never really harmed anyone, but they were up to many kinds of mischief. Sometimes a hunter, picking up his cap in the morning, would find the feathers plucked out. Sometimes a fisherman, missing his paddle, would discover it at last in a tree. When such things happened it was perfectly plain that Puk-Wudjies had

been up to their pranks and few persons were still stupid enough to believe it could be anything else.

Neen-i-zu had her own ideas concerning these little men, for she, like Morning Glory, had often listened to the tales that old Iagoo told. One of these stories was the story of a Happy Land, a far-off place where it was always summer, where no one wept or suffered sorrow.

It was for this land that she sighed. It filled her thoughts by day when she sought the secret places of the hills and sat in some lonely spot, listening to the mysterious voices that whispered in the breeze. Where was this Happy Land—this place without pain or care?

Tired at night, she would sink into her bed. Then from their hiding places would come stealing the small messengers of Weenz, the Spirit of Sleep. These kindly gnomes—too small for the human eye to see—crept quickly up the face of the weary Neen-i-zu and tapped gently on her forehead with their tiny war clubs, called *pub-ga-mau-guns*. Tap—tap—tap—until her eyelids closed and she sought the Happy Land in the other pleasant land of dreams.

She, too, had seen the footprints of the Puk-Wudjies on the sandy beach of the little lake and had heard their merry laughter ring out in the grove of pines. Was it their only dwelling place? she asked herself. Or were they not messengers from the Happy Land, sent to show the way to that mortal who believed in it and longed to enter?

Neen-i-zu came to think that this must be really so. Oftener than ever she made her way to the meadow bordering on the Spirit Wood and sat there gazing into the grove. Perhaps the Puk-Wudjies would understand and tell the fairies whom they served. Then some day a fairy would appear at the edge of the pines and beckon her to come. That would surely happen, she thought, if she wished it long enough and could give her wishes wings. So, sitting there, she composed the words of a song and set it to the music the pines make when the south wind stirs their branches. Then she sang:

Spirit of the laughing leaves,
Fairy of the forest pine,
Listen to the maid who grieves
For that happy land of thine.
From your haunt in summer glade
Hasten to your mournful maid.

Was it only her fancy that she seemed to hear the closing words of her song echoed from the deep woods where the merry little men had vanished? Or was it the Puk-Wudjies mocking her?

She had lingered later than usual. It was time to go. The new moon swung low in the western sky, its points turned upward to the heavens. An Indian would say he could hang his powder horn upon it and that it meant dry weather, when the leaves crackled under the hunter's feet and the animals fled before him, so that he was unable to come near enough to shoot. And Neen-i-zu was glad of this. In the Happy Land, she declared, no one would suffer and no life would be taken.

Yet it was a hunter that her mother wished her to marry, a man who spent his whole life slaying the red deer of the forest, who thought and talked of almost nothing else.

This came into her mind as she rose from her seat in the meadow and cast a farewell glance at the pines. The rays of the crescent moon touched them with a faint light and again her fancy came into play. What was it that seemed to move along the edge of the mysterious woods? Something with the dim likeness of a youth—taller than the Puk-Wudjies—who glided rather than walked and whose garments of light green stood out against the darker green of the pines. Neen-i-zu looked again, but the moon hid behind the hills. All was black to the eye. To the ear came no sound but the creepy cry of the whippoorwill. She hastened home.

That night she heard from her mother's lips what she had long expected and feared. "Neen-i-zu," said her mother. "I named you 'My Dear Life,' and you are as dear as life to me. That is why I wish you to be safe and happy. That is why I wish you to marry a good man who will take the best care of you now and will protect and comfort you when I am gone. You know the man I mean."

"Yes, Mother," answered Neen-i-zu. "I know him well enough—as well as ever I want to know him. He hunts the deer, he kills the deer, he skins the deer. That is all he does, that is all he thinks, that is all he talks about. It is perhaps well that someone should do this, lest we starve for want of meat. Yet there are many other things in the world and this hunter of yours is content if he does but kill."

"Poor child!" said her mother. "You are too young to know what is best for you."

"I am old enough, Mother dear," answered Neen-i-zu, "to know what my heart tells me. Besides, this hunter you would have me marry is as tall as a young oak, while I am not much taller than one of the Puk-Wudjies. When I stand up very straight, my head comes little higher than his waist. A pretty pair we would make!"

What she said was quite true. Neen-i-zu had never grown to be much larger than a child. She had a graceful, slender body, little hands and feet, eyes black as midnight, and a mouth like a meadow flower. One who saw her for the first time, passing upon the hills, her slight figure sketched against the sky, might have thought that she herself was a fairy.

For all her gentle, quiet ways and her love of lonely places, Neen-i-zu was often merry. But now she seldom laughed. Her step was slow and she walked with her eyes fixed upon the ground.

When she is married, thought her mother, she will have other things to occupy her mind, and she will no longer go dreaming among the hills.

But the hills were her one great joy—the hills, and the flowery meadows where the lark swayed to and fro, bidding her be of good cheer, as he perched on a mullein stalk. Every afternoon she sat, singing her little song. Soon she would sing no more. The setting sun would gild the pine grove, the whippoorwill would complain to the stars, but the picture would be incomplete. There would be no Neen-i-zu. For the wedding day was named; she must be the hunter's wife.

On the day set for her marriage to the man she so disliked, Neen-i-zu put on the garments of a bride. Never had she looked so lovely. Blood-red blossoms flamed in her jet-black hair. In her hand she held a bunch of meadow flowers mingled with the tassels of the pine.

Thus arrayed, she set out for a farewell visit to the grove. It was a thing they could not well deny her. But as she went her way, and the hills hid her from sight, the wedding guests looked uneasily at one another. It was something they could not explain. At that moment a cloud blew up from nowhere, across the sun. Where light had been there was now a shadow. Was it a sign? They glanced sidelong at the hunter, but the bridegroom was sharpening his sheath knife on a stone. Sunshine or shadow, his thoughts were following the deer.

Time passed, but Neen-i-zu did not return. Then so late was the hour that the wedding guests wondered and bestirred themselves. What could be keeping her so long? At last they searched the hills. She was not there. They tracked her to the meadow, where the prints of her little moccasins led on and on—into the grove itself. Then the tracks disappeared. Neen-i-zu had vanished.

They never saw her again. The next day a hunter brought them strange news. He had climbed a hill on his way home by a shortcut, and had paused there a moment to look around. Just then his dog ran up to him, whining, its tail between its legs. It was a brave dog, he said, that would not run from a bear, but this one acted as if he had seen something that was not mortal.

Then the hunter heard a voice, singing. Soon the singing

stopped, and he made out—far off—the figure of Neen-i-zu, walking straight toward the grove, her arms held out before her. He called to her, but she did not hear, and drew nearer and nearer to the Spirit Wood.

"She walked like one who dreams," said the hunter, "and when she had almost reached the woods, a young man, slender as a reed, came out to meet her. He was not one of our tribe. No, no! I have never seen his like. He was dressed in the leaves of the forest and green plumes nodded on his head. He took her by the hand. They entered the Sacred Grove. There is no doubt that he was a fairy— the fairy Evergreen. There is nothing more. I have finished.

So Neen-i-zu became a bride, after all.

The

Red Swan

nce, a long, long time ago, there were three brothers who were left on their own when their parents died. The eldest hunted for food as best he could, and with the provisions stocked by their parents they managed to get along. They did not even have neighbors to lend them a helping hand, for their father had withdrawn from the tribe many years before and had lived with his family in a solitary place. The boys had no idea if other people lived nearby. They did not even know who their parents had been, for at the time of their death even the eldest was quite young.

Alone as they were, they nevertheless were in good spirits. They took advantage of every opportunity and, in time, learned how to hunt. The eldest brother became expert in the craft of the forest and he was very successful in procuring food. He was skillful in killing buffalo, elk, and moose, and he taught his brothers so that they, too, could hunt for food and take care of themselves.

One day the elder brother declared that he wanted to leave and go in search of the world, but promised to return and bring back wives for the three of them. His brothers, however, refused to let him go.

Jeekewis, the second, was loud in his disapproval of the idea. "We have lived so long by ourselves," he said. "We can still do without wives." This argument prevailed, and for a time the three brothers continued together.

One day they each agreed to kill a male animal for the purpose of making quivers from the skins. When these quivers were prepared they were immediately filled with arrows, for the brothers all had a feeling that something was about to happen for which they must be ready.

Soon after this they hunted on a wager to see who would come in first with game. They set out on different paths. Maidwa, the youngest, had not gone far before he saw a bear. He followed the animal closely and, driving an arrow through him, brought him to the ground.

Maidwa began skinning the bear when suddenly the air all around him was tinted with red. He rubbed his eyes, thinking he was perhaps deceived. But rub as hard as he would the red hue still colored the air and tinged with delicate splendor every object that he looked at—the treetops, the river that flowed before him, and the deer that glided along the edge of the forest.

As he stood musing about this spectacle, a strange distant noise came to his ears. At first it seemed like a human voice. Following the sound he reached the shore of a lake. Floating at a distance upon its waters sat a most beautiful red swan, its plumage glittering in the sunlight. When the swan lifted its neck it uttered the peculiar cry he had heard. He was within long bowshot, and, drawing the arrow to his ear, he took careful aim and discharged the shaft. It had no effect. The beautiful bird sat proudly on the water still pouring forth its peculiar chant, still spreading the radiance of its plumage and lighting the whole world with its ruby splendor.

Maidwa shot again and again, until his quiver was empty, for he longed to possess so glorious a creature. But the swan, untouched, did not even spread its wings to fly. Circling round and round, it stretched its long neck and dipped its bill into the water, as if indifferent to the arrows of a mortal.

Maidwa ran home and brought back all the arrows in the lodge, which he shot at the swan. Finally, he stood with his bow at his side, lost in wonder, gazing at the beautiful bird.

While standing thus, eagerly longing for the possession of their fair swan, Maidwa remembered his elder brother saying that in their dead father's medicine sack there were three magic arrows. But his brother had not told Maidwa that their father, on his death-bed, had bequeathed these arrows to his youngest son, Maidwa. The thought of the magic arrows excited Maidwa and he hastened with all speed to get them.

At any other time he would have hesitated to open his father's medicine sack, but something prompted him to believe that it was not wrong to open it now. Snatching the arrows he ran back, not staying to return the other contents to the sack but leaving them scattered about the lodge.

Maidwa feared that the swan must by this time have taken wing. But as he emerged from the wood he found to his great delight that the air was as rosy as ever and there, serene and beautiful, sat the glorious red swan.

With trembling hand Maidwa shot the first of his magic shafts. It grazed a wing. The second came closer and cut away a few of the bright red feathers, which fluttered and fell like flakes of fire in the water. The third arrow, which he carefully aimed and drew home upon the string with all his force, made the lucky hit and passed through the neck of the bird a little above the breast.

"She is mine," cried Maidwa. But to his great surprise, instead of drooping its neck and drifting to the shore, the red swan flapped its wings, rose slowly, and flew majestically toward the falling sun.

Maidwa, that he might meet his brothers with a good face, rescued two of the magic arrows from the water. And although the swan had carried off the third, he hoped to recover that one, too, and be master of the magnificent bird.

Maidwa was noted for his speed. He would shoot an arrow and then run so fast that the arrow always fell behind him. He now set off, running as fast as he could.

I can run fast, he thought, and I can catch the swan.

He sped over hills and prairies toward the west. He was thinking about seeking a place to sleep for the night, when, suddenly, he heard distant noises like the murmur of waters against the shore. As he ran on he heard voices and soon he saw people, some of whom were busy felling trees, the strokes of their axes echoing through the woods. He passed them and when he emerged from the forest the sun was just falling below the edge of the sky.

Maidwa was determined to find the swan, whose red track he marked well far westward until she was lost to sight. Meanwhile he would stop for the night and find something to eat, since he had had neither food nor drink since he left home.

At a distance, on rising ground, he could see the lodges of a large village. He went toward it and soon heard the voice of the watchman, who stood on a height to overlook the place and give notice of the approach of friends or foes.

"We are visited," the watchman cried, and a loud halloo indicated that all had heard him.

When Maidwa advanced, the watchman pointed to the lodge of the chief. "It is there you must go," he said and left him.

"Come in, come in," said the chief. "Take a seat there." He pointed to the side of the lodge where his daughter sat. "It is there you must sit."

He was given some food and a few questions were put to him because he was a stranger. It was only when he spoke that the others answered.

"Daughter," said the chief, as soon as the night had set in, "take our son-in-law's moccasins and see if they be torn. If they are so, mend them for him."

Maidwa thought it strange that he should be so warmly received and instantly married against his own wishes, although he could not help noticing that the chief's daughter was very pretty.

It was some time before she picked up the moccasins which he had taken off. It displeased him to see her hesitate to do so. When at last she did reach for them, he snatched them from her hand and hung them up himself. He lay down and thought of the swan and made up his mind to leave with the dawn.

He awakened early. Finding the chief's daughter standing at the door, he spoke to her, but she did not reply. He touched her arm lightly.

"What do you want?" she said and turned her face away from him.

"Tell me," said Maidwa, "what time the swan passed. I am following it. Come outside and point the way."

"Do you think you can overtake it?" she said.

"Yes," he answered.

"*Naubesah*—fool!" retorted the chief's daughter.

She went out, however, and pointed in the direction he should go. The young man loped along slowly until the sun rose. Then he began traveling at his accustomed speed. He spend the day running, and although he could not see the red swan anywhere on the horizon, he thought that he discerned a faint red light far over in the west.

When night came he was pleased to find himself near another village. When still at a distance he heard the watchman crying out,

"We are visited," and soon the men of the village came out of their lodges to see the stranger.

He was again told to enter the lodge of the chief and his reception was in every respect the same as on the previous night. Except this young woman was even more beautiful than the first and she entertained him very kindly. Although Maidwa was urged to stay with them, he was determined to continue his journey and capture the red swan.

Before daybreak he asked the young woman what time the red swan had passed, and to point the way the swan had gone. She marked against the sky with her finger the course the swan had taken and told him that it had passed yesterday when the sun was between midday and its falling place.

Maidwa again set out rather slowly, but when the sun had risen he tested his speed by shooting an arrow ahead and running after it. It fell behind him and he knew that he had lost none of his quickness of foot.

Nothing remarkable happened through the day and he continued leisurely. Some time after dark, as he was peering around the country for shelter, he saw a light coming from a small low lodge. He went up to it very slyly, and, peeping through the door, he saw an old man alone, his head down upon his breast, warming his back before the fire.

Maidwa thought that the old man did not know that he was standing near the door, but he was mistaken, for, without turning his head to look at him, the old man said, "Walk in, my grandchild. Take a seat opposite me, and take off your things and dry them, for you must be tired. I will prepare something for you to eat. You shall have something very delicate."

Maidwa accepted this kind invitation and entered the lodge. The old man then remarked, as if in the simple course of conversation, "My kettle with water stands near the fire."

Immediately, a small earthen pot with legs appeared near the fire. The old man then took one grain of corn and one grain of whortle-berry and put them into the pot.

Maidwa was very hungry and seeing the limited scale of the old man's housekeeping he thought his chance to have a good supper was slight. The old man had promised him something very delicate and he seemed likely to keep his word. But Maidwa looked on silently, and did not change the expression on his face any more than if a great banquet was being prepared.

The pot soon boiled, whereupon the old man said quietly, "The pot will stand at a distance from the fire."

The pot removed itself and the old man said to Maidwa, "My grandchild, feed yourself," and handed him a dish and ladle of the same ware as the pot itself.

The young man, whose hunger was very great, helped himself to all that was in the pot. He felt ashamed to think that he had done so, but before he could speak the old man said, "Eat, my grand-child, eat, eat!" A few minutes later he again said, "Help yourself from the pot."

Maidwa was surprised, on dipping in his ladle, to see that the pot was full. And although he emptied it a second time, it was again filled and refilled until his hunger was entirely satisfied.

The old man then said, without raising his voice, "The pot will return to its corner." And the pot went back to its accustomed placed in an out-of-the-way corner of the lodge.

Maidwa observed that the old man was about to address him and took an attitude that showed that he was prepared to listen.

"Keep on, my grandchild," said the old man. "You will surely gain that which you seek. To tell you more I am not permitted, but go on as you have begun and you will not be disappointed. To-morrow you will again reach an old man, but it is the one you will see after him who will tell you all, and will explain the manner in which you must proceed to accomplish your journey. Often has this red swan passed, and those who have followed it have never returned. But you must be firm in your resolution and be prepared for all that may happen."

"So will it be," answered Maidwa, and they both lay down to sleep.

Early in the morning the old man ordered his magic pot to prepare breakfast so that his guest might eat before leaving. As Maidwa left, the old man gave him a blessing with his parting advice.

Maidwa set forth in better spirits than at any other time since he had started. Nightfall found him in company with another old man, who had a frisky little kettle that hurried up to the fire before it was spoken to, bustled about and set supper briskly before Maidwa, and then hurried away again, without waiting for orders. This old man entertained him kindly and also carefully directed him on his way in the morning.

Maidwa traveled with a light heart, since he now expected to meet the old man who was to tell him how to proceed to capture the red swan.

Toward nightfall Maidwa reached the lodge of the third old man. Before coming to the door he heard him saying, "Grandchild, come in." And going in he promptly felt quite at home.

The old man prepared something for him to eat, acting as the others had done. His kettle was of the same size and looked as if it were a brother of the two others that had fed him, except that this kettle, in coming and going about its household duties, would make a passing remark or sing a little tune.

The old man waited until Maidwa had fully satisfied his hunger before he addressed him. "Young man, the errand you are bound on is beset with trials and difficulties. Numbers have passed with the same purpose as that which now prompts you, but they never returned. Be careful and if your guardian spirits are powerful you may succeed. This red swan you are following is the daughter of a magician who has an abundance of everything, but only this one child whom he values more than the sacred arrows. In former times he wore a cap of wampum, which was attached to his scalp. But powerful Indians, warriors of a distant chief, came and told him that their chief's daughter was dying and that she herself requested his wampum cap, which she was confident would save her life. 'If I can only see it,' she said, 'I will recover.' It was for this cap they had come and at length the magician consented to part with it, in hope that it would restore to health the dying maiden, although when he took it off to hand it to the messengers it left the crown of his head bare and bloody.

"Years have passed since then and his head has not healed. The coming of the warriors to procure the cap for the sick maiden was a cheat. They are now constantly making sport of the unhappy scalp—dancing it about from village to village—and with every insult it receives the poor old magician to whom it belongs groans with pain. Those who hold it are too powerful for the magician. Many have sacrificed themselves to recover it for him, but without success.

"The red swan has enticed many a young man, as she has you, to enlist them to procure the scalp. Whoever is so fortunate as to succeed, it is understood, will receive the red swan as his reward.

"In the morning you will proceed on your way. Toward evening you will come to this magician's lodge. You will know it by the groans which you will hear far over the prairie as you approach. He will ask you in. You will see no one but the magician. He will question you about your dreams and the strength of your guardian spirits. If he is satisfied with your answers he will urge you to attempt the recovery of his scalp. He will show you the course to take. If you feel inclined, as I see that you shall, go forward, my grandson, with a strong heart. Persevere, and I have a strong feeling that you will succeed."

Maidwa answered, "I will try."

Early in the morning he set off again on his journey, after having eaten from the magic kettle which sang a kind of farewell chant on its way from the fireplace to its station in the corner.

Toward evening, as he crossed a prairie, Maidwa heard groans from a distant lodge, which were only interrupted by a voice from a person whom he could not see, calling to him, "Come in! Come in!"

As the young man entered the lodge the man who Maidwa realized must be the magician heaved a great groan from the very bottom of his chest. Maidwa saw that the crown of his head was all bare and bloody.

"Sit down, sit down," the magician said, "while I make you something to eat. You see how poor I am. I have to attend to all my own wants, with no servant other than that poor little kettle in the corner. Kettle, we will have something to eat, if you please."

"In a moment," the kettle spoke up from the corner.

"You will oblige me by making all the haste you can," said the magician, in a humble tone, still addressing the kettle.

"Have patience," replied the kettle, "and I will be with you presently."

After a considerable delay, there came forward out of the corner from where it had spoken a great heavy and potbellied kettle, which advanced with much stateliness and solemnity of manner until it was directly in front of the magician, whom it addressed with the question, "What shall we have, sir?"

"Corn, if you please," the magician answered.

"No, we will have whortleberries," replied the kettle in a firm voice.

"Very well. Just as you choose."

When he supposed it was time, the magician invited Maidwa to help himself.

"Wait a minute," interposed the kettle, as Maidwa was about to dip in his ladle. He paused, and after a delay, the kettle, shaking itself up and simmering very loudly, said, "Now we are ready."

Maidwa fell to and satisfied his hunger.

"Will the kettle now withdraw?" asked the magician, with an air of much deference.

"No," said the kettle, "we will stay and hear what the young man has to say for himself."

"Very well," said the magician. "You see," he added to Maidwa, "how poor I am. I have to take counsel with the kettle or I should be all alone without a day's food and with no one to advise me."

All this time the red swan was carefully concealed in the lodge, behind a curtain from which Maidwa heard now and then a rustling noise that fluttered his spirits and set his heart to beating at a wonderful rate.

As soon as Maidwa had partaken of food and laid aside his leggings and moccasins, the old magician began telling how he had lost his scalp, the insults it was receiving, the pain he suffered thereby, his wishes to regain it, the many unsuccessful attempts that had already been made, and the numbers and power of those who retained it. He would interrupt his discourse at times with sudden groans, and say, "Oh, how shamefully they are treating it."

Maidwa listened to all the old magician had to say with solemn attention.

The magician renewed his discourse and asked Maidwa about his dreams, or what he saw in his sleep, at such times as he had fasted and darkened his face to procure guardian spirits.

Maidwa then told him one dream. The magician groaned.

"No, that is not it," he said.

Maidwa told him of two or three others.

The magician groaned again and again and said, rather peevishly, "No, these are not the dreams."

"Keep cool," said the kettle. It had left the fire and was standing in the middle of the floor where a pleasant breeze was blowing through the lodge. Then it added, "Have you no more dreams of another kind?"

"Yes," said Maidwa, and he told him one.

"That will do," said the kettle. "We are much pleased with that."

"Yes, that is it—that is it!" the magician added. "You will cause me to live. That was what I was wishing you to say. Will you then go and see if you cannot recover my poor scalp?"

"Yes," said Maidwa, "I will go. And the day after tomorrow, when you hear the ka-kak cries of the hawk, you will know that I am successful. You must prepare your head and lean it out through the door, so that the moment I arrive I may replace your scalp."

"Yes, yes," said the magician. "As you say it will be done."

Early the next morning Maidwa set out to fulfill his promise. In the afternoon, when the sun hung toward home, he heard the shouts of a great many people. He was in a wood at the time, and saw, as he thought, only a few men, but as he went on they increased in numbers. When he emerged upon the plain, their heads appeared like the hanging leaves, they were so many.

In the middle of the plain he saw a post and something waving at its top. It was the wampum scalp. And every now and then the air was rent with the war song, for they were dancing the war dance in high spirits around it.

Before he could be seen, Maidwa said some magic words that the magician had told him and changed himself into a hummingbird. He flew toward the scalp. When he passed some of those who were standing nearby, he came close to their ears. As they heard the rapid whirr that this bird makes when it flies, they jumped aside and asked each other what it could be. Maidwa by this time had almost reached the scalp, but fearing that he might be seen while untying it, he now changed himself into the down that floats lightly on the air, and sailed slowly on to the scalp. He loosened it, and moved off with difficulty, since the weight was almost too great for him to carry. The Indians around would have snatched it away had not a lucky current of air just then buoyed him up. As they saw that the scalp was moving away they cried out, "It is taken from us! It is taken from us!"

Maidwa was borne gently along a little way above their heads. As they followed him, the rush and hum of the people was like the beating of the surges upon a lake shore after a storm. But the good wind, gaining strength, soon carried him beyond their pursuit. A little further on he changed himself into a hawk and flew swiftly off with his trophy, crying, "Ka-kak! ka-kak!" until the shrill hawk cry resounded far and wide.

Meanwhile, the magician remembered Maidwa's instructions and placed his head outside the lodge as soon as he heard the cry of the hawk.

In a moment Maidwa came past with rustling wings, and as he flew he gave the magician a severe blow on the head with the wampum scalp. The old man's limbs quivered in pain, but the scalp adhered just as Maidwa, in his own body, walked into the lodge and sat down, feeling perfectly at home.

The magician was so long in recovering from the stunning blow that had been dealt him that Maidwa feared he had destroyed his life when he restored the crown of his head. Presently, however, he was pleased to see the magician show by the motion of his hands and limbs that his strength was returning. In a little while he stood up. And to Maidwa's delight he beheld, instead of a withered old man far advanced in years and stricken in sorrow, a bright and cheerful youth who stood before him gleaming with life.

"Thank you, my friend," the young magician said. "Your kindness and bravery have restored me to my former body."

They embraced and the young magician urged Maidwa to stay for a few days. Maidwa was glad to accept this invitation and the two young men quickly formed a strong attachment to each other.

The magician, however, to Maidwa's deep regret, never once alluded to the red swan.

At last the day arrived when Maidwa prepared to return to his home. The young magician bestowed on him ample presents of wampum, fur, robes, and other costly things. Although Maidwa was yearning to see the red swan, to hear her spoken of, and to learn what his fortune was to be in regard to that fond object of his pursuit, he controlled his feelings and never so much as looked in the direction where he supposed she might be. His friend observed the same silence and caution.

Maidwa's pack for traveling was now ready and he was having his farewell smoke when the young magician said to him, "My friend Maidwa, you know the reason that you came so far, and why you have risked so much and waited so long and so patiently. You have, indeed, proved to be my friend. You have accomplished your goal and your noble perseverance shall not go unrewarded. If you undertake other tasks with the same spirit you will always succeed. My destiny compels me to remain where I am, although I should be happy to be allowed to go with you. I have given you, of ordinary gifts, all you will need as long as you live. But I see you yearn to speak of the red swan. I appreciate your delicacy, but I vowed that whoever procured my lost wampum-scalp for me should be rewarded by possessing her."

He then spoke in a language which Maidwa did not understand. The curtain of the lodge parted and Red Swan met his delighted gaze. It was a beautiful maiden that he beheld, so majestic and airy in her appearance that he seemed to see a creature whose home should be in the heavens, among the rosy clouds, rather than in this dim lodge.

"Take Red Swan," the young magician said. "She is my sister. Treat her well. She is worthy of you and what you have done for me merits more. She is ready to go with you to your kin and friends. My good wishes shall go with you both."

Red Swan smiled kindly at Maidwa, who advanced and greeted her. Hand in hand they left the lodge and, watched by the young magician, walked across the prairie on their homeward course.

They traveled slowly and looked with joy at the beautiful countryside over which they had both so lately passed with hearts ill at ease.

After two or three days they reached the lodge of the third old man, who had entertained Maidwa with the singing kettle. But the kettle was not there. The old man, nevertheless, received them very kindly and said to Maidwa, "You see what your perseverance has secured you. Persevere always and you will succeed in whatever you undertake."

The following morning, when they were about to leave, the old man pulled from the side of the lodge a bag, which he presented to Maidwa, saying, "Grandchild, I give you this. It contains a present for you and I hope you will live happily to an old age."

Bidding him farewell, they again set out on their journey.

That night they came to the second old man's lodge. He, too, gave them a present and bestowed his blessing. Although he looked, Maidwa saw nothing here of the frisky little kettle that had been so lively on his former visit.

They journeyed on until they came to the lodge of the first old man. There their reception was the same, except when Maidwa glanced at the corner he failed to see the silent kettle, which had served him so well. The old man smiled when he realized the direction of Maidwa's glance, but he said nothing.

When, on continuing their journey, they at last approached the first town that Maidwa passed in his pursuit, the watchman gave notice as before and Maidwa was shown into the chief's lodge.

"Sit down here, son-in-law," said the chief, pointing to a place near his daughter. "And you, too," he said to Red Swan.

The chief's daughter was engaged in dying some fabric, and quite indifferent to these visitors, she did not even raise her head. Presently the chief said, "Let someone bring in our son-in-law's traveling pack."

When the pack was laid before him, Maidwa opened one of the bags that it contained. The bag was filled with various costly articles—wampum, robes, and trinkets of much riches. These he presented to the chief as a token of his regard. The chief's daughter stole a glance at the costly gifts, then at Maidwa and his beautiful wife. She stopped working and was silent and thoughtful all evening. The chief himself talked with Maidwa of his adventures, congratulated him on his good fortune, and concluded by telling him that he should take his daughter along with him when he left in the morning.

"It will be a pleasure to do so," replied Maidwa.

The chief then spoke up, saying, "Daughter, be ready to go with him in the morning. You will marry one of his brothers."

At peep of day amid the good wishes of their new friends, Maidwa, Red Swan, and the chief's daughter took their leave.

Toward evening they reached the other town where Maidwa had spent a night. The watchman gave the signal and men, women, and children came out to see them. They were again shown into the chief's lodge. The chief welcomed Maidwa, saying, "Son-in-law, you are welcome." He asked Maidwa to take a seat next to his daughter, and the two women did the same.

After suitable refreshments for all, Maidwa smoked a pipe and the chief asked him to relate his adventures in the hearing of everyone who had gathered in the lodge.

Maidwa told them his whole story. When he came to those parts that related to Red Swan they turned and looked upon her in wonder and admiration, for she was very beautiful.

The chief then told Maidwa that his brothers had been to their town in search of him, but that they had gone back some time before, having given up all hopes of ever seeing him again. "But you are a man of spirit," the chief continued, "whom fortune is pleased to befriend. Take my daughter with you and marry her to one of your brothers. So shall we be more closely bound together."

When at last Maidwa was about to leave he gave rich presents to the chief and invited members of the chief's family to go with him and visit his hunting grounds, where he promised they would find game in abundance. They consented and in the morning a large company assembled and joined Maidwa. And the chief, with a party of warriors, escorted them a long distance. When the chief was ready to return, he made a speech and sought the blessing of the Good Spirit on Maidwa, his family and his friends.

The two companies parted, marching away over the prairie, each one its own course, their waving feathers glittering in the morning sun, their war drums sounding afar.

After several days' travel, Maidwa and his friends came in sight of his home. The others rested in the woods while he went alone to see his brothers.

He entered the lodge. All was in confusion and the floor was covered with ashes. On one side, sitting among the cinders, was his elder brother. His face was blackened and he was crying aloud. On the other side sat the younger, Jeekewis, also with a blackened face, his head covered with stray feathers and tufts of swan's down. He looked so odd that Maidwa could not keep from laughing. But Jeekewis seemed to be so lost in grief that he did not notice his brother's arrival. The eldest brother, however, lifted his head and recognized Maidwa. Then he jumped up, shook his hands, kissed him, and expressed much joy at his return. Indeed, they had been convinced that Maidwa was dead and had for several weeks been mourning him.

Maidwa explained that he had returned with many gifts and had brought each of his brothers a wife. Now Jeekewis was roused. He ran to the door and peeped out to see the strangers. He then began jumping and laughing and crying out "Women! women!" and that was all the reception he gave his brother.

Maidwa told his brothers to wash themselves and put the lodge in order while he unpacked his traveling pack. Among the riches the young magician had bestowed upon him was the large talking kettle. In the bag the third old man had given him he found the wonderful singing kettle. The present the second old man had given him was the frisky little kettle. And the gift from the first old man was the large silent kettle. What wonderful presents these are, thought Maidwa.

While Maidwa unpacked, Jeekewis scampered about and began to wash himself. But every now and then, with one side of his head all feathers and the other clean and shining, he would peep out to look at the women again. "I will have that one," he said. "No, I will have that one."

As soon as order was restored Maidwa went out to bring all the women and his other friends in. When everyone was seated Maidwa said, "These women were given to me to dispose of in marriage. I now give one to each of you." He then presented the first chief's daughter to his eldest brother.

Maidwa led the other daughter to Jeekewis and said, "My brother, here is a wife for you. Live happily."

Jeekewis hung his head as if he were ashamed, but he would every now and then steal a look at his wife and also at the other women. By and by he turned toward his wife and acted as if he had been married for years. Maidwa, seeing that no preparation had been made to entertain the company, said, "Are we to have no supper?"

He had no sooner spoken than from a corner stepped the silent kettle, which placed itself by the fire and began bubbling and boiling quite briskly. Presently this kettle was joined by the big talking kettle, which said, addressing itself to Maidwa, "Master, we shall be ready presently." And then, dancing along, there came from still another corner the frisky little kettle, which hopped to their side and took part in the preparations of the evening meal. When all was nearly ready, a delicate voice was heard singing in the last corner of the lodge. Keeping up its dainty carol all the way to the fireplace, the fourth kettle joined the three cooks.

It was not long before the big kettle advanced toward Maidwa and said, in his confident way, "Supper is ready!"

The feast was a jovial one, for they were all hungry, and plied their ladles with right good will. And yet the four magic kettles were always full no matter how often they were dipped into.

Maidwa and his friends lived in peace for some time. Each had a lodge and their community prospered. There was no lack of children and everything else was in abundance.

But one day the two brothers began to look darkly at Maidwa. They reproached him for having taken from the medicine sack their dead father's magic arrows. They upbraided him especially because one was lost.

After listening to them in silence, Maidwa said that he would go in search of the lost arrow and that it should be restored. The very next day, true to his word, he left them.

After traveling a long way and looking in every direction, almost without hope of discovering the lost treasure, he came to an opening in the earth. When he descended into this, a path led him to the abode of departed spirits. The countryside was beautiful, the pastures were greener than his own, the sky bluer than that which hung over the lodge, and the extent of it was lost in a dim distance. Moreover he saw animals of every kind wandering about in great numbers. The first he came to were buffaloes. His surprise was great when they spoke to him.

They asked him what he came for, how he had descended, and why he was so bold as to visit the abode of the dead.

He answered that he was in quest of a magic arrow, to appease the anger of his brothers.

"Very well," said the leader of the buffaloes. "We know it," and he and his followers moved off a little from Maidwa, as if they were afraid of him. "You have come," resumed the buffalo spirit, "to a place where a living man has never before been. Return immediately to your family, for under pretense of recovering one of the magic arrows that belong to you by your father's dying wish, your brothers have sent you off so that they may become possessed of your beautiful wife, Red Swan. Speed home! You will find the magic arrow at the lodge door. You will live to a very old age and die happily. You can go no farther in these abodes of ours."

Maidwa looked, as he thought, to the west, and saw a bright light as if the sun was shining in its splendor, but he saw no sun.

"What light is that yonder?" he asked.

The leader of the buffaloes answered: "It is the place where those who were good dwell."

"And that dark cloud?" Maidwa again asked.

"It is the place of the wicked," replied the buffalo.

This cloud was very dark and to look upon it hurt his eyes.

With the help of his guardian spirits Maidwa returned to the earth again and beheld the sun giving light as usual. All else that he learned in the abode of the dead is unknown, for he never spoke of it to any human being.

After regaining the earth and wandering a long time to gather knowledge to make his people happy and to add to their comfort, he drew near his village one evening. Passing all the other lodges he came to his own door, where he found the magic arrow as he had been promised. He heard the loud voices of his brothers. They were arguing about which one would have possession of Red Swan, who had remained constant all the time Maidwa was away and sadly awaited his return. Maidwa listened in shame and sorrow.

He entered the lodge holding his head high and shining with anger. He spoke not a word, but placed the magic arrow in his bow, and would have laid his brothers dead at his feet, but just then the talking kettle stepped forward and spoke such words of wisdom that Maidwa laid down his bow. The singing kettle trolled forth such a soothing little song, the guilty brothers were so contrite and keenly repentant of their intended wrong, Red Swan was so radiant and forgiving, the silent kettle immediately served them so hearty and wholesome a meal, and the frisky little kettle was so joyful and danced about so merrily, that Maidwa decided to forgive them. And when the magic arrows were laid away in the medicine sack there was in all the Indian country that night no happier family than the three brothers, who ever after dwelt together in all kindness, as all good brothers should.

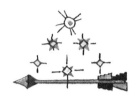

How the
Summer Came

orning Glory was tired of the winter and longed for the spring to come. Sometimes it seemed as if Ka-bib-on-okka, the fierce old North Wind, would never go back to his home in the Land of Ice. With his cold breath he had frozen tight and hard Big-Sea-Water, Gitche Gumee, and covered it deep with snow until you could not tell the great lake from the land. Except for the bright green pines, all the world was white—a dazzling, silent world in which there was no musical murmur of waters and no song of birds.

"Will O-pee-chee, the robin, never come again?" sighed Morning Glory. "Suppose there was no summer anywhere, and no Sha-won-dasee, the South Wind, to bring the violet and the dove. Oh, Iagoo, would it not be dreadful?"

"Be patient, Morning Glory," answered the old man. "Soon you will hear Wa-wa, the wild goose, flying high up on his way to the north. I have lived many moons. Sometimes he seems long in coming, but he always comes. When you hear him call, then O-pee-chee, the robin, will not be far behind."

"I'll try to be patient," said Morning Glory. "But Ka-bib-on-okka, the North Wind, is so strong and fierce. I can't help wondering whether there ever was a time when his power was so great that he made his home here always. I shiver to think of it!"

Iagoo rose from his place by the fire, and drew to one side the curtain of buffalo hide that screened the doorway. He pointed to the sky—clear and sparkling with stars.

"Look!" he said. "There, in the north. See the little cluster of stars. Do you know the name we give it?"

"I know," said Eagle Father. "It is O-jeeg An-nung—the fisher stars. If you look right, you can see how they make the body of the fisher. He is stretched out flat, with an arrow through his tail. See, sister!"

"The fisher," repeated Morning Glory. "You mean the furry little animal, something like a fox? Is 'marten' another name for it?"

"That's it," said Eagle Feather.

"Yes, I see," nodded Morning Glory. "But why is the fisher spread out flat that way, in the sky, with an arrow sticking through his tail?"

"I don't know just exactly why," admitted Eagle Feather. "I suppose some hunter was chasing him. Perhaps Iagoo can tell us."

Iagoo closed the curtain and went back to the fire.

"You thought there might have been a time when there was no summer on the earth," he said to Morning Glory. "And you were right. Until O-jeeg, the fisher, found a way to bring the summer down from the sky, the earth was everywhere covered with snow and it was always cold. If O-jeeg had not been willing to give his life so that all the rest of us could be warm, Ka-bib-on-okka, the North Wind, would have ruled the world as he now rules the Land of Ice."

Then Morning Glory and Eagle Feather sat down on the soft rug that was once the winter coat of Muk-wa, the bear, and Iagoo told them the story of How the Summer Came:

In the wild forest that borders the Great Lake there once lived a mighty hunter named O-jeeg. No one knew the woods so well as he. Where others would be lost without a trail to guide them, he found his way easily and quickly, by day or night, through the trackless tangle of trees and underbrush. Where the red deer fled, he followed. The bear could not escape his swift pursuit. He had the cunning of the fox, the endurance of the wolf, the speed of the wild turkey when it runs at the scent of danger.

When O-jeeg shot an arrow, it always hit the mark. When he set out on a journey, no storm or snow could turn him back. He did everything he said he would do, and he did it well.

Thus it was that some men came to believe the O-jeeg was a Manito—the Indian name for one who was magic powers. This much was certain: whenever O-jeeg wished to do so, he could change himself into the little animal known as the fisher, or marten.

Perhaps that is why he was on such friendly terms with some of the animals, who were always willing to help him when he called upon them. Among these were the otter, the beaver, the lynx, the badger, and the wolverine. There came a time, as we shall see, when he needed their services badly and they were not slow in coming to his assistance.

O-jeeg had a wife whom he dearly loved, and a son, of thirteen years, who promised to be as great a hunter as his father. Already he had shown great skill with the bow and arrow. If some accident should prevent O-jeeg from supplying the family with the game upon which they lived, his son felt sure that he himself could shoot as many squirrels and turkeys as they needed to keep them from starving. With O-jeeg to bring them venison, bear's meat, and wild turkey, they had thus far plenty to eat. Had it not been for the cold, the boy would have been happy enough. They had warm clothing,

made from deerskin and furs. To keep their fire burning, they had all the wood in the forest. Yet, in spite of this, the cold was a great trial; for it was always winter and the deep snow never melted.

Some wise old men had somewhere heard that the sky was not only the roof of our own world, but also the floor of a beautiful world beyond; a land where birds with bright feathers sang sweetly through a pleasant, warm season called Summer. It was a pretty story that people wished to believe. And likely enough, they said, when you came to think that the sun was so far away from the earth and so close to the sky itself.

The boy used to dream about it and wonder what could be done. His father could do anything. Some men said he was a Manito. Perhaps he could find some way to bring Summer to the earth. That would be the greatest thing of all.

Sometimes it was so cold that when the boy went into the woods his fingers would be frostbitten. Then he could not fit the notch of his arrow to the bowstring and was obliged to go back home without any game whatever. One day he had wandered far in the forest and was returning empty-handed, when he saw a red squirrel seated on his hind legs on the stump of a tree. The squirrel was gnawing a pine cone, and did not try to run away when the young hunter came near.

Then the little animal spoke: "My grandson," said he, "there is something I wish to tell you that you will be pleased to hear. Put away your arrows and do not try to shoot me, and I shall give you some good advice."

The boy was surprised, but he unstrung his bow and put the arrow in his quiver.

"Now," said the squirrel," listen carefully to what I have to say. The earth is always covered with snow and the frost bites your fingers and makes you unhappy. I dislike the cold as much as you do. To tell the truth, there is little enough for me to eat in these woods with the ground frozen hard all the time. You can see how thin I am, for there is not much fat in a pine cone. If someone could manage to bring the Summer down from the sky, it would be a great blessing."

"Is it really true, then," asked the boy, "that up beyond the sky is a pleasant warm land, where Winter only stays for a few moons?"

"Yes, it is true," said the squirrel. "We animals have known it for a long time. Ken-eu, the war eagle, who soars near the sun, once saw a small crack in the sky. The crack was made by Way-wass-i-mo, the Lightning, in a great storm that covered all the earth with water. Ken-eu, the war eagle, felt the warm air leaking through. But the people who live up above mended the crack the very next moment and the sky has never leaked again."

"Then our wise old men were right," said the boy. "O-jeeg, my father, can do most anything he has a mind to do. Do you suppose if he tried hard enough he could get through the sky and bring the Summer down to us?"

"Of course!" exclaimed the squirrel. "That is why I spoke to you about it. Your father is a Manito. If you beg him hard enough, and tell him how unhappy you are, he is sure to make the attempt. When you go back, show him your frostbitten fingers. Tell him how you tramp all day through the snow and how difficult it is to make your way home. Tell him that some day you may be frozen stiff and never get back at all. Then he will do as you ask, because he loves you very much."

The boy thanked the squirrel and promised to follow this advice. From that day he gave his father no peace.

At last O-jeeg said to him, "My son, what you ask me to do is a dangerous thing and I do not know what may come of it. But my power as a Manito was given to me for a good purpose and I can put it to no better use than to try to bring the Summer down from the sky and make the world a more pleasant place to live in."

Then he prepared a feast to which he invited his friends the otter, the beaver, the lynx, the badger, and the wolverine. And they all put their heads together to decide what was best to be done. The lynx was the first to speak. He had traveled far on his long legs and had been to many strange places. Besides, if you had good strong eyes, and you looked at the sky on a clear night when there was no moon, you could see a little group of stars which the wise old men said was exactly like a lynx. It gave him a certain importance, especially in matters of this kind. So when he began to speak, the others listened with great respect.

"There is a high mountain," said he, "that none of you has ever seen. No one ever saw the top because it is always hidden by the clouds, but I am told it is the highest mountain in the world and almost touches the sky."

The otter began to laugh. He is the only animal that can do this. Sometimes he laughs for no particular reason, unless it is that he thinks himself more clever than the other animals, and likes to show off.

"What are you laughing at?" asked the lynx.

"Oh, nothing," answered the otter. "I was just laughing."

"It will get you into trouble some day," said the lynx. "Just because you never heard of this mountain, you think it is not there."

"Do you know how to get to it?" asked O-jeeg. "If we could climb to the top, we might find a way to break through the sky. It seems a good plan."

"That is what I was thinking," said the lynx. "It is true I don't know just where it is. But a moon's journey from here, there lives a Manito who has the shape of a giant. *He* knows, and he could tell us."

So O-jeeg bade good-bye to his wife and his little son and the next day the lynx began the long journey with O-jeeg and the others following close behind. It was just as the lynx had said. When they had traveled, day and night, for a moon, they came to a lodge, as the white men call an Indian's tent; and there was the

Manito standing in the doorway. He was a queer-looking man, such as they had never seen before, with an enormous head and three eyes, one eye set in his forehead above the other two.

He invited them into the lodge and put some meat before them. But he had such an odd look and his movements were so awkward that the otter could not help laughing. At this the eye in the Manito's forehead grew red, like a live coal, and he made a leap at the otter, who barely managed to slip through the doorway, out into the bitter cold and darkness of the night, without having tasted a morsel of supper.

When the otter had gone the Manito seemed satisfied, and told them they could spend the night in his lodge. They did so and O-jeeg, who stayed awake while his friends slept, noticed that only two of the Manito's eyes were closed while the one in his forehead remained wide open.

In the morning the Manito told O-jeeg to travel straight toward the North Star, and that in twenty suns—the Indian name for days—they would reach the mountain. "As you are a Manito yourself," he said, "you may be able to climb to the top and to take your friends with you. But I cannot promise that you will be able to get down again."

"If it is close enough to the sky," answered O-jeeg, "that is all I ask."

Once more they set out. On their way they met the otter, who laughed again when he saw them. But this time he laughed because he was glad to find them and glad to get some meat that O-jeeg had saved from the Manito's supper.

In twenty days they came to the foot of the mountain. Then up and up they climbed, until they passed quite through the clouds. Up once more, until at last they stopped, all out of breath, and sat down to rest on the highest peak in the world. To their great delight, the sky seemed so close that they could almost touch it.

O-jeeg and his comrades filled their pipes. But before smoking they called out to the Great Spirit, asking for success in their attempt. In Indian fashion they pointed to the earth, to the sky overhead, and to the four winds.

"Now," said O-jeeg, when they had finished smoking, "which of you can jump the highest?"

The otter grinned.

"Jump, then!" commanded O-jeeg.

The otter jumped and, sure enough, his head hit the sky. But the sky was the harder of the two and back he fell. When he struck the ground he began to slide down the mountain. Soon he was out of sight and they saw him no more.

"Ugh!" grunted the lynx. "He is laughing on the other side of his mouth."

It was the beaver's turn. He, too, hit the sky, but fell down in a heap. The badger and the lynx had no better luck and their heads ached for a long time afterward.

"It all depends on you," said O-jeeg to the wolverine. "You are the strongest of them all. Ready, now—jump!"

The wolverine jumped and fell, but came down on his feet, sound and whole.

"Good!" cried O-jeeg. "Try again!"

This time the wolverine made a dent in the sky.

"It's cracking!" exclaimed O-jeeg. "Now, once more!"

For the third time the wolverine jumped. Through the sky he went, passing out of sight, and O-jeeg quickly followed him.

Looking around them they beheld a beautiful land. O-jeeg, who had spent his life among the snows, stood like a man who dreams, wondering if it could be true. He had left behind him a bare world, white and winter, whose waters were always frozen, a world without song or color. He had now come into a country that was a great green plain with flowers of many hues, where birds of bright plumage sang amid the leafy branches of trees hung with golden fruit. Streams wandered through the meadows and flowed into lovely lakes. The air was mild and filled with the perfume from a million blossoms. It was Summer.

Along the banks of a lake were the lodges in which lived the people of the sky, who could be seen some distance away. The lodges were empty, but before them were hung cages in which there were many beautiful birds. Already the warm air of Summer had begun to rush through the hole made by the wolverine, and O-jeeg now made haste to open the cages, so that the birds could follow.

The sky dwellers saw what was happening and raised a great shout. But Spring, Summer, and Autumn had already escaped through the opening into the world below, and many of the birds as well.

The wolverine, too, had managed to reach the hole and descend to the earth before the sky dwellers could catch him. But O-jeeg was not so fortunate. There were still some birds remaining that he knew his son would like to see, so he went on opening the cages. By this time the sky dwellers had closed the hole and O-jeeg was too late.

As the sky dwellers pursued him, he changed himself into the fisher and ran along the plain, toward the North, at the top of his speed. In the form of the fisher he could run faster. Also, when he took this shape, no arrow could injure him unless it hit a spot near the tip of his tail.

But the sky dwellers ran even faster and the fisher climbed a tall tree. They were good marksmen and they shot a great many arrows until at last one of these chanced to hit the fatal spot. Then the fisher knew that his time had come.

Now he saw that some of his enemies were marked with the totems, or family arms, of his own tribe. "My cousins!" he called to them. "I beg of you that you go away and leave me here alone."

The sky dwellers granted his request. When they had gone, the fisher came down from the tree and wandered around for a time, seeking some opening in the plain through which he might return to the earth. But there was no opening. At last, feeling weak and faint, he stretched himself flat on the floor of the sky, through which the stars may be seen from the world below.

"I have kept my promise," he said with a sigh of content. "My son will now enjoy the summer, and so will all the people who dwell on the earth. Through the ages to come I shall be set as a sign in the heavens, and my name will be spoken with praise. I am satisfied."

So it came about that the fisher remained in the sky, where you can see him plainly for yourself on a clear night, with the arrow through his tail. The Indians call them the fisher stars—O-jeeg An-nung. But to white men they are known as the constellation of the plow.

JOHN RAE